Not Alone on the Voyage

Not *Alone* on the *Voyage*

Anne-Marie Jennings

iUniverse

NOT ALONE ON THE VOYAGE

iUniverse books may be ordered through booksellers or by contacting:

iUniverse
1663 Liberty Drive
Bloomington, IN 47403
www.iuniverse.com
1-800-Authors (1-800-288-4677)

ISBN: 978-1-4917-9952-9 (sc)
ISBN: 978-1-4917-9954-3 (hc)
ISBN: 978-1-4917-9953-6 (e)

Print information available on the last page.

iUniverse rev. date: 08/11/2016

Chapter 1

The moment the wheels of the plane touched down in Inuvik, Sandy was convinced she had made a terrible mistake.

Her feelings of dread had actually begun nearly four hours ago, when she realized that she was going to have to walk outside and step on the tarmac in order to get on the plane. The cool breeze hit her face as she began to climb the steps into the small 30-seater plane that would take her to Inuvik. Sandy had never been this far west in her life, and once she reached her final destination for the day, she would be farther north than she ever imagined she would ever go.

She had never been asked to choose between the fish and the caribou for her in-flight meal, and she'd never overheard someone say the weather might make landing in Norman Wells impossible. In her experience, flying had always been about walking along the warm gateway protected from the elements, getting into the seat and arriving at her destination—pure and simple. Thinking about the weather or the ability to land had never been a factor. Another first on this trip had been when they landed in Yellowknife to pick up some additional passengers, Sandy was asked to deplane while they refuelled. But by this point, there was no turning back now.

Once the plane left Yellowknife and began its voyage farther north, Sandy reached into her carry-on bag to make sure the diary was still there. That diary was the sole reason she was taking this trip. Losing it now would have been her undoing.

Ever since the day she had found it three weeks ago, the brown leather-encased notebook had never left her possession. It sat on the kitchen table while she ate, it was on the couch beside her when she was watching the news, and it had been safely tucked under her pillow while she slept.

The diary was now the only link she had to her husband, Jack. It contained the last story of his life she would ever learn, and in many ways it was currently the only thing that gave her a reason to get up in the morning. Without having had Jack's words to read, Sandy would have probably given up.

Sandy still missed her husband every day, and she would for as long as she lived. She knew he would have supported her taking this trip, and she felt his presence so strongly that it was almost as if he was sitting in the empty seat beside her.

But he wasn't, and he never would be.

The announcement that they were about to land in Inuvik forced Sandy back to reality. She turned to look out the window, hoping to see a little bit more of the town, but all she saw was barren land—nothing to give her any kind of comfort. From what she could see, the rocky terrain didn't make trying to live here any easier. What on earth was it about this place that made Jack call it one of his favourite places on the planet?

Once the plane touched down and began taxiing down the airstrip, Sandy realized she would have to continue on her journey, primarily because there were no more flights to Edmonton until tomorrow afternoon.

Sandy stepped off the plane, crossed the tarmac and walked through the door (she couldn't bring herself to call it a gate) of the Inuvik airport. As she took up a spot beside the conveyor belt to wait for her luggage, Sandy took a quick look around. She could not stop staring at the stuffed polar bear in the centre of the airport, or at the impressive photographs of fishing and hunting that were on every wall. As foreign as the terminal seemed to her, Sandy was strangely comforted by the sounds of mobile phones while her fellow passengers received calls or checked their text messages.

The terminal was so small that Sandy could hear the customer service agents at the Canadian North counter talking to one of the airport workers about the latest item of hot gossip in town and then asking about their plans for the weekend. Sandy had to stifle her laughter when she heard the sounds of a nervous young man getting up the courage to ask the pretty blonde customer service agent to spend Saturday night with him.

The bags came creeping along the conveyor belt, with Sandy's being one of the last to appear. Entirely unfamiliar with how people travelled in the North, she had arrived at the Edmonton airport extremely early, and she was pretty sure she had been the first person to check in for the day's flight.

Bag in hand, Sandy took a deep breath and headed for the exit door. Not sure how long it would take her to get to her hotel, she was pleasantly surprised to find four cabs waiting to pick up anyone who needed a ride. She walked over to the first car in the line-up and gave her suitcase to the driver, who was already standing at the back of the car and holding open the trunk.

Still somewhat overwhelmed, Sandy quietly climbed into the back seat. A few minutes passed before she realized the cab driver was talking to her. He said, "You haven't heard a word I've said, have you?"

"I'm sorry," Sandy said. "It's been a very long day already, and this is the first time I have felt as if I could finally start to relax."

"That's okay. Why don't you tell me where I'm going? You'll be able to relax as much as you want soon enough."

Sandy smiled apologetically while reaching into her pocket for her itinerary. "I'm staying at … the Eskimo Inn."

The cab driver nodded quickly and put the car in gear. As they drove away from the airport, Sandy settled back in her seat. She watched the dusty highway towards Inuvik unfold in front of her eyes and knew she wasn't going to be able to relax just yet.

"So how are you enjoying your first visit up North?" the cab driver asked.

"How did you know this was my first visit?"

"It's pretty obvious. You have been looking like a deer caught in the headlights since I saw you come out of the airport. That, and the fact that you haven't been listening to me one bit since you told me where you're staying."

"I really am sorry. I've had a lot on my mind since I began this trip very early this morning. I'm not usually rude—it's simply a case of overthinking things."

"So what brings you to Inuvik?" the cabbie asked.

"I'm not really staying in Inuvik all that long. I'm on my way to Holman."

"Holman? That's quite a place to visit on your very first trip here. Why Holman?"

"Let's just say I'm trying to find a friend."

Satisfied with her response, the cab driver went back to the task of bringing Sandy into town. Jack pines lined the road for kilometres. The majestic mountain hills only served to highlight the feelings of isolation for Sandy, and it was becoming pretty clear that she was never going to be able to truly relax on this trip.

"How long have you lived here?" Sandy asked the cab driver.

"Let's see. It's been six years since I moved here from Edmonton. My brother was already here, and I decided I needed a change of scenery. I couldn't have really asked for a more extreme change of scenery."

"Do you think you're going to stay here much longer?"

"I don't know. To be honest, I've never really thought much about it. I was never planning on staying this long. Well, here we are. Welcome to the town of Inuvik."

The cab reached the top of a large hill, and Sandy got her first look at Inuvik.

A large structure was covered in red and blue steel.

"That's the regional hospital," the cabbie noted.

There were row upon row of brightly coloured houses. "People call those the smartie box houses. I live in that blue one on the left."

A second building was covered in corrugated steel, this time in light blue. "That's the post office."

A traffic light.

A Catholic church in the shape of an igloo.

And finally, a white stone building with a blue sign.

"Here you go. The Eskimo Inn."

"This is it?" Sandy asked.

The cab driver turned around to look at her. "Well, it's not the Hilton, but it's about the best place to stay around these parts. The restaurant isn't too shabby either."

"Of course," Sandy said, slightly embarrassed by her knee-jerk reaction. "I guess I really didn't know what to expect, but obviously it was something different."

"No problem. I've seen worse reactions. At least you're not begging me to take you back to the airport."

"Does that actually happen?"

He grinned. "Sometimes. But when I tell them the next flight to Edmonton isn't until tomorrow afternoon, they ask me how much for the ride and get out."

Sandy smiled. "So how much do I owe you?"

"It's twenty-five dollars."

Sandy fumbled around in her purse to find her wallet. She pulled out three ten-dollar bills, and handed them to the driver. "Here you go. Keep the change."

The driver smiled brightly. "Thanks."

Sandy opened the door to get out of the cab. As she walked to the trunk, she was surprised to find the driver had gotten out to help her. Again Sandy chastised herself for not expecting better from people. *Must be a big-city thing*, she thought.

The cabbie said, "I hope you enjoy your visit."

"My visit? What makes you think I'm going to stay?"

"Well, I've seen a lot of people come and go here. I have developed a pretty good sense for knowing who's going to stay and enjoy themselves, and who is going to go back home and have missed out completely. You don't strike me as someone who wants to miss out."

As the cab driver jumped back into his vehicle and drove away, Sandy was left to ponder his last comment. She had to admit to herself that he wasn't actually wrong, because in a way that was why she had made the trip from Ottawa in the first place.

Standing on the sidewalk outside the hotel, Sandy took a good look around. The sign across the street pointing out a bank was a familiar sight—and reminded Sandy she needed to get some extra cash before leaving Inuvik tomorrow morning. Dusty pickup trucks and SUVs lined both sides of the street, and even though it was only 3:30 in the afternoon, there weren't too many people on the street.

Sandy had never been farther away from home in her life—and she'd never felt more alone.

After taking a deep steadying breath, she picked up her suitcase and walked up the front steps and into the hotel. She approached the check-in desk and noticed the desk clerk was too wrapped up in a gossip magazine to notice whether someone was standing in front of her. After waiting patiently for a few minutes, Sandy cleared her throat to get the clerk's attention.

"Oh," the clerk said sheepishly as she threw her magazine down. "I'm so sorry! I just get wrapped up in silly stuff sometimes."

"It's no problem. A well-written article can do that to you."

The clerk chuckled. "I'm not sure well-written is the best way to describe it, but I appreciate you saying as much. I take it you have a reservation?"

"Yes. Stonehouse."

"Oh, right. You were coming in on the flight from Edmonton today. How was it?"

"The flight? It was okay," Sandy said.

"Good. Sometimes the turbulence can be pretty brutal. Did you manage to land in the Wells?"

"We landed in Yellowknife for about an hour. And we did land somewhere else for about thirty minutes."

"Then you did manage to land in Norman Wells today. That's good. Sometimes the flight can't land because of weather, so I was curious."

"But it's July."

The clerk nodded, handing Sandy her room key. "Mother Nature doesn't discriminate. You're in room 225. You can either take the stairs behind you, or the elevator at the end of the hall to your right."

"Thanks. I hear you have a pretty good restaurant."

"It's not bad; they serve a decent burger. If you're feeling brave, there are a couple of restaurants on this street that aren't too far away."

"I think I'll stick nearby. Thanks for the information."

"I hope you enjoy your stay in Inuvik."

"Thanks. I actually won't be staying all that long. I'm on my way to Holman tomorrow."

The clerk looked surprised. "Really? Well, I hope the weather holds out for you."

The telephone rang, and the desk clerk ended the conversation with Sandy and went back to business.

Sandy picked up her suitcase and headed up the stairs. She was tired. Two days of cabs and planes and hotels, and more planes and more cabs and more hotels, took a lot out of a person. When one factored in the deep sadness and loneliness, not to mention the time change, travelling to Inuvik was that much more taxing.

Coming this far was a big step on the journey, but it was really only the latest stop. Tomorrow would be the really big step.

Sandy opened the door to her room and tossed her carry-on on a blue armchair, and she put her suitcase on the bed. She took a quick look around to better orient herself. It was a very institutional-looking room: cinder-block walls painted white, a drab grey carpet on the floor, a bedspread covering a double bed that matched the drapes, an old television, a small alarm clock, a telephone Sandy had seen in a thousand different offices over the years and a window that offered a view of the generator for the building.

Turning away from the window, Sandy headed to the armchair where she had dropped her carry-on. After finding her husband's diary once more, Sandy sat down on the bed and flipped the pages to the first entry.

As she started to read, Sandy backed up to lean against the headboard.

How can they do this to me? After I spent the last three weeks making big plans for this summer with my buddies and getting up the courage to tell my parents about said plans, they tell me they've arbitrarily decided to send me away. According to them, "It will be a summer like none other."

Of course the summer they had planned was going to be like none other. I was going to be absolutely miserable. I was going to be away from home, away from my friends, in the middle of nowhere and absolutely miserable. I don't think I'll ever be able to forgive them for this one.

What's even worse is that I'll be so far from civilization it's not even funny. If they wanted to send me to a small town for the summer, fine; at least I'd be able to get to a big city fairly easily. But they're sending me to a small town north of the 60ᵗʰ parallel with no road in whatsoever. There aren't even regular flights out of there.

When they said they were going to send me to the middle of nowhere, I thought that they were sending me to somewhere within driving distance of home—not somewhere that required three days of flying to reach. From the moment I stepped off the plane, people have been staring at me, and I've never felt more uncomfortable in my entire life.

I'm never going to forgive them for this … I'll never be able to forget what they've done to me.

Although Sandy had already read the first few entries, the pain was just as strong for her the second time around. Wiping the tears from her face, she headed for the bathroom to throw some cold water on her face. She took a look at herself in the mirror.

Five years. All she'd had was five years.

In the cosmic scheme of things (at least according to Sandy), five years had not nearly been long enough.

There was still so much she wanted—and needed—to know about her husband. Finding a diary detailing the events of a summer before she'd ever met Jack proved that fact to her. In many ways, finding the diary had been a stroke of pure luck, because it blended in quite well with all the other books in Jack's den she was throwing into a big box to take to the used bookstore. But for some reason, Sandy felt compelled to pull it out of the pile and take a closer look, and she was glad she had. Now she had one more trip to take with Jack, and he would help her find the strength to go on. But that would have to wait until after she took a quick nap. Sandy stepped out of the bathroom and sat down on the bed. The moment her head hit the pillow, she was fast asleep.

Three hours later, Sandy awoke with a start. She had forgotten that she was in Inuvik, and it took her a few minutes to reorient herself and get her breathing back under control. Realizing what time it was and that she hadn't eaten since the meal on the flight from Edmonton, she decided to try her luck on the hotel lounge.

She grabbed Jack's diary and left the room on her way to dinner. When she opened the door to the lounge, Sandy walked over to a small table in the corner and sat down. There weren't too many people eating in the lounge, which meant that Sandy would no doubt have some peace and quiet while eating. She decided to keep reading Jack's diary.

She turned to the second entry.

Chapter 2

Holman.

The place is appropriately named, because it's a hole, man.

I still can't believe I'm stuck here for the summer. My father told me that when he was my age, his father did the same thing to him, and his life was never the same after that. I can only imagine that this is some sort of family torture handed down from father to son simply because it was done to one, and the rest of us are still paying for the consequences.

This is probably the smallest place I have ever seen. I did some reading up on this town before I left, and I really think my parents must truly hate me to send me to a place like this. From what I have learned, it doesn't take much more than 20 minutes to walk around and see everything there is to see. The population is only a couple of hundred people, very few of whom aren't aboriginal, and there doesn't seem to be any type of industry in this place.

I can't imagine living here for too long, and it's shocking to think there are people in this place who have never left in their entire lives. At least I know there is a light at the end of the tunnel, and I'll get out of here someday in the near future.

I'm actually north of the Arctic Circle.

I'm certainly not supposed to be here. In the great plan for the rest of my life, Holman did not figure in any way whatsoever.

I tried to reason with my father; I tried to tell him this was a big mistake. But he was already decided on how I was going to spend my summer, and there was no way I was going to get out of it. He said he'd never thought of sending me this far away from home, but when the opportunity fell into his lap, he couldn't resist.

If you ask me, I don't see how spending three months in the middle of nowhere is a good idea. Summer holidays are supposed to be about hanging out with your buddies and getting into all kinds of trouble in the place you grow in—not to spend your time in a town on the shore of the Arctic Ocean.

I'll have to make sure I punch out whoever it was who gave my father this crazy idea in the first place. Of course he claims he's doing it for my own good, but I'm not about to prove to him that I'm not the kind of person who can deal with this. I'm not about to have him tell me, "I told you so," when I get back to civilization.

I've made up my mind. Instead of sitting around in this rustic outpost and feeling sorry for myself, I am going to try to make something out of this experience.

Maybe then my father will take notice of me.

Sandy was wiping the tears from her eyes when the server finally came over with a menu. "I hope you don't think I was ignoring you. You looked like you were deep in thought, and I didn't want to interrupt."

"Thanks. I appreciate it, "Sandy said as she blew her nose in her paper napkin.

"Are you okay, miss?"

Sandy nodded. "I'm fine. Just a little bit sad these days."

"I'm sorry to hear that. I'll just tell you that our special tonight is a steak sandwich and leave you to make your decisions. Can I get you something to drink?"

"How about just a cup of coffee?"

The server nodded quickly and left Sandy to her sadness. It was clear that Sandy didn't really need anyone to ask her too many questions, and the server wasn't too interested in small talk with someone who was only passing through town. Clearly the woman had seen more than her share of people coming and going.

For her part, Sandy appreciated that she was left alone. The people were nice enough, but they didn't seem too interested in poking their noses into her business. Sandy chalked a lot of that up to people not really knowing her, but she wasn't sure she would want too many people asking her questions right now, because she knew she didn't have any answers.

Tomorrow was the next step in getting her answers. Jack had found all his answers in Holman, and Sandy hoped she would be able to do the same.

From her pocket, Sandy pulled out a piece of paper with all the information about Holman she could find, and she took another look. Even with the words in front of her, Sandy could still not believe what she was reading. She had done a little bit of research about where she was going before she left, but there weren't too many books on Holman on the shelves. She had even asked the librarian for help, but it was clear Sandy had found all the books that the librarian would have recommended. She had called the travel agent to book a ticket, it took three days before the agent was able to figure out the itinerary.

All in all, it wasn't much information. Barely enough to fill up one sheet of letter-sized paper. It was not a whole lot of information to go on considering Sandy was taking the biggest risk in her entire life. She knew this was a big risk, but she knew she had to follow this out to the end, no matter what happened. There had been more than a few people who were of the opinion she was making a terrible mistake—that in her grief and sorrow, Sandy was making some awful choices, like leaving town. Even her closest friends weren't as supportive as they could have been when it counted.

Take Alison, for example. As Sandy's best friend since university, Alison had always been the one person on whom Sandy knew she could rely. But even Alison couldn't understand what she wanted to do and why. "Sandy, I'm sorry," Alison said as she reached out her hand to grab her friend's arm. "I know how much your heart is breaking, and I know better than to tell you to just get over Jack's death and move on."

Sandy stopped dead in her tracks and heaved a sigh. When she turned around to face Alison, she already had tears streaming down her cheeks. "It's not fair, Allie. I'm not supposed to be a widow yet. I should have spent the last few days planning our summer vacation, not trying to find a way to move on without my husband."

"Honey, it wasn't as if anyone could have known that Jack was going to get killed in a car accident by a drunk driver. If anyone had known, don't think he would have done everything he could have to save Jack?"

Sandy wiped the tears from her face. "I want to believe that, Allie. People have been telling me that everything happens for a reason. If that's true, I have a hard time believing that tearing my heart into shreds is a part of the master plan of the universe."

Alison pulled Sandy over to the curb so they could sit down and talk. Although she hadn't said anything, Alison knew Sandy had not been sleeping or eating well since Jack's death. Alison had tried a number of times to step in and help out, but she was afraid to overstep her boundaries and do something Sandy would not appreciate.

"I can't do this anymore," Sandy said.

"What do you mean? What are you talking about?"

"This. I can't keep up the appearance of being strong. Alison, I don't have the energy anymore."

"You're starting to scare me, San. I don't like to hear you talk this way. Let's go inside, have a cup of tea and talk about this somewhere more comfortable than the front seat of my car."

"Everyone tells me I am strong enough to go on without Jack. Everyone tells me that I'll be a better person for having gone through this experience, that I'll grieve and mourn and then be able to move on. Well, you know what? I don't want to be strong. I don't want to find a way to go on without Jack. I don't want to be better for the experience, and I don't want to be able to move forward with my life. I can't see myself going through the motions for the rest of my life."

Alison was beginning to panic. The pain in Sandy's voice was almost too much to bear, and Alison realized for the first time just how heartbroken Sandy was and how much her friend was truly hurting. For the second time since she'd returned home with Sandy, Alison was afraid.

Alison said, "You know you can't give up. I know everything seems hopeless right now, but you have to hold on tight to the belief that things will only get better."

"That's where you're wrong, Allie. Without Jack, nothing will ever get better. That's why I'm going away."

"You're leaving?

"Yes. I can't stay here surrounded by my memories of Jack and my dreams of a wonderful life we will never have."

"But where are you going to go?

Sandy pulled the diary out of her briefcase. Alison couldn't stifle her gasp, stunned by just how wrong she had been about her friend's healing. Sandy was in a worse state than Alison had thought.

"Sandy," Alison said nervously. "What exactly are you talking about? What is that book?"

"This diary tells of the summer before I met Jack. According to what he wrote in this book, it was the best summer of his life—yet he never mentioned it once. I'm going to find out what Jack learned the summer before he met me. He said it made him the man I fell in love with, and that's a place I have to see for myself."

Alison knew there was no talking her friend out of this one. As crazy as the idea to go off on her own may have been, Sandy needed to find closure. If Sandy was to find the courage and the strength to live in a world without Jack, she had to truly know everything about the man who was her husband, good or bad. Her friend was strong and had a stubborn streak a mile wide; Alison knew she couldn't argue.

Sandy shook her head and smiled weakly. She had been expecting this type of initial reaction, but she had hoped her best friend would have understood her need to go. Alison had always appeared to be on the same wavelength as Sandy, but her reaction proved Sandy wrong.

Sandy said, "I thought of all people, you would understand the why. Staying here is only going to kill me slowly. Everywhere I turn, all I can think of is a time when Jack and I went to this place or that place, or how Jack used to love to tell me stories about fishing when he was a boy in the creek behind his parents' house, or the time he fell out of the tree in the park."

"Let me get this straight. You want to drop everything, leave all your friends and family behind when you probably need them the most and fly to some God-forsaken part of the country because you want to find about what Jack did when he was there?"

"I thought you guys were right. I thought that time would make it easier. But the truth is time is only making things worse. Every day I find myself feeling a little more heartbroken, a little bit more certain that moving on will be virtually impossible if I stay here. If I do stay here, Allie, I'll die for sure. You have to let me go."

As Sandy stood up and headed into the kitchen for another cup of coffee, she heaved a heavy sigh of despair. "I was really hoping you'd understand my reasons, Allie. I thought you'd be in my corner at least."

"What on earth are you talking about? Did you honestly think I'd support a trip like this? You're pointing at a place above the Arctic Circle, for Pete's sake!"

"No one else understands why I have to go. Every other person I've told about my plans has told me I was crazy to go visit a place at the end of the world simply because my husband wrote that at some point in his life, he was sent there by his parents because they thought it was a good idea. You have no idea just how demoralizing it is to watch people you thought would love and support you in your greatest time of need look at you with disappointment and incomprehension."

Alison stood up to approach Sandy. The look in Sandy's eyes was enough to tell Alison what she needed to know. As much as she feared for her friend, there was nothing she could do to change her mind. All Sandy wanted was Alison's support.

Alison felt her conviction begin to crumble, because she was starting to believe Sandy was right. The grief Sandy was feeling over Jack's death was only crippling her, and Alison knew Sandy's recovery could only happen in a place where she wouldn't be reminded of her dead husband. If she wanted her best friend to survive, she was going to have to let her go—or sit back and watch Sandy die. Alison was afraid to let Sandy go, but she also knew there was really nothing else she could do to change her friend's mind.

"Sandy, I'm sorry. I know that if this is something you need to do, then I'm completely behind you. While I might not really understand your reason for going away, I should at least be wise enough to know that you have no choice but to go."

"You have no idea how badly I needed you to say those words, Allie. I was beginning to think no one would understand."

"I'm not saying I really understand what you want to do, but I know you wouldn't think about it unless you felt you had to. If all you need is for someone to listen to you, then that's exactly what I'll do for you."

"That's all I need. This trip is going to be hard enough without having to explain myself to everyone."

Alison wanted to support her friend's plan to venture into northern Canada, but she had some reservations that simply wouldn't go away. She knew Sandy needed to find closure in her own way and time, yet the potential for additional disaster was still very much in the forefront of Alison's thoughts. Her best friend had just lost the love of her life. What if going into unknown territory led to more pain and heartache? She knew there was no way she could dissuade Sandy, and she secretly hoped that her friend would come to her senses before there was no turning back.

But Alison had always been a lousy poker player, and Sandy knew the truth. She knew her friend didn't believe she was doing the right thing, and she also knew Alison was saying things she thought Sandy needed to hear. Alison's feigned support hurt more than if Alison had been honest with her friend about her disapproval.

"You know, Alison, if you think I'm making a mistake, I really wish you'd just be big enough to tell me as much."

"Look, I can't say you're wrong, because I think you're about to make a terrible mistake. Running off to God knows where isn't the answer."

"Do you honestly think losing Jack is something I'm just going to get over? There's no getting over the loss of the other half of my soul, even if I were to live to 105! I'm not even sure I *want* to get over it."

Alison was now worried. "What does that mean?"

"That means I'm not sure I want to become someone who doesn't remember everything about Jack. I don't want to become someone who can simply move on after having spent every single day with one person. I don't want to open the closet to look for a sweater when I'm cold and not find his clothes in there. I don't want to forget what his favourite beer is. I don't want to watch a football game and not hear him calling the penalties before the referee throws the flag."

"Then why the hell are you planning on leaving all that behind and flying off to some God-forsaken part of the country, just because you think it will help you better understand a man you claim you already know better than anyone else in the world?"

Sandy let the tears flow freely down her cheeks. "I don't have a choice in the matter, Alison. When I found the diary, I felt as I had been given a second chance to learn all about the only man I have ever loved all over again. This is something I never knew about Jack, but if what he says is true, this is what made him the man I wanted to be with until my dying day. This place he spent a summer in is the one place that changed his whole life for the better, and I think I need to see it for myself."

"Are you sure about this, Sandy?"

Sandy wiped a defiant hand across her face. "I've already decided I'm going, whether or not anyone likes the idea. I need to do this."

After what had felt like an eternity to Sandy, Alison finally got the message.

"So … do you need a ride to the airport?"

Chapter 3

Sandy's mind returned to the present day. She tried to think about what Jack must have been feeling all those years ago when he was on the same trip. Back then, the flights and the condition of the planes flying to the Arctic must have been even more precarious than they were today, and Jack had not had much experience with the outside world when he was headed to Holman. Jack had always lived a pretty sheltered life while in his parents' home, and there were times during the early years of their marriage that Sandy found herself wondering just how he had managed to get along without her before they met.

The ache in her chest became too much. Having finished her dinner, Sandy charged her meal to her room and left the lounge behind her. She returned to her room, tucked Jack's diary under the pillow and headed to the bathroom to take a shower. Allowing the warm water to cascade over her aching muscles, Sandy cried bit more in the shower, secure in knowing that no one was going to ask her if she was okay as she stepped out.

Sandy dried her hair, stepped out of the bathroom and took her pyjamas out of her suitcase. Although it was still pretty early, the only thing Sandy really wanted to do was to crawl into bed and sleep. She had a feeling that she was going to need all the strength she could get to help here through the next phase of her journey

I don't know how these people live in a place where you can't even get a decent meal. I've had enough meat and rice and bread and anything but a good salad to last me for a while. I won't even say just how far I am from the closest fast-food restaurant, but I've been told that trip would take me a couple of days and a few flights.

When I make a comment about that geographic reality, most of the locals sit back and laugh. They say they've seen a thousand people just like me pass through town, and they'll no doubt see at least a thousand more in their lifetimes. Most people in these parts are very transitory and have no problems with picking up stakes and moving for a couple of months, or even a couple of years when the spirit hits them.

Take Charlie, for example. Charlie is the guy I've been spending the bulk of my time with so far, and I still haven't figured out exactly why it is he chooses to stay here. He's a smart guy is and really handy; if he wanted to, he could have a job anywhere in this country and make a pretty good living. Apparently, he and my father met years ago when my father was working in Edmonton on some construction job, so I guess Charlie had his ticket out of here, and he chose to throw it away. I can't imagine giving up a chance a good life to come back here for any reason. Charlie could be anywhere he wanted to be in this world.

But he's here, hell and gone from what most people would consider civilization, and he swears up and down that he doesn't want to live anywhere else in the world. He says he tried to live in the big city for a while, but he was so miserable and homesick that he sold all his stuff and had enough money for a one-way ticket to Holman. He's never looked back.

That was almost 20 years ago, and Charlie has never had the desire to try his luck in southern Canada again. He says he's staying put, he belongs right here.

I envy him. I wish sometimes I knew where I was supposed to be ...

The feelings of dread Sandy had felt when she landed in Inuvik returned the next day when the customer service agent asked her to step on to the scale with her suitcase.

"You want me to stand on the scale?"

The young man smiled brightly. "You want to go to Holman today? You have to get on the scale. Everyone does it—even Junior over there."

She looked in the direction the man was pointing. In the corner she saw a great hulk of a man, who had to be more than six feet tall and 300 pounds. Regarding that nickname went, he was far from being junior at all.

"His name is Junior? That's a bit ironic, isn't it?"

"You should see his dad."

Laughing, Sandy got up on the scale with her suitcase. The young man wrote some numbers down on his register and nodded to Sand. She stepped off the scale and found a seat in the corner across from Junior.

As it had upon her arrival in Inuvik yesterday, the stuffed polar bear in the centre of the airport building captured her attention. Sandy wondered about how the bear got there in the first place, and she also wondered whether she was going to see one in the flesh. But if she did, she knew she would probably not survive a real-life encounter.

After about half an hour of people watching and waiting, the flight to Holman was announced. The small group of people in the airport began heading out the door to the smallest plane Sandy had ever seen. The 12-seater turboprop plane reminded her of the radio-controlled planes her brother used to play with as a young boy.

She lined up with the other passengers but didn't understand why no one was going up the steps. "What are we waiting for?" she asked one of the other passengers.

"Bobby's trying to balance out the plane. No one can get on until he figures out who gets to sit where."

"Really?"

The passenger nodded. "Absolutely. If the plane isn't as balanced as possible, we could end up in the ocean."

Not understanding the logic behind the balancing but afraid to ask any more questions, Sandy continued to wait patiently. Oddly enough, she wasn't surprised to see Junior get on the plane first.

Ninety minutes later, the small plane landed in Holman. Sandy hadn't looked out the window much during the flight because she didn't want to ruin the surprise. Oddly enough, she did not feel as awkward climbing out of the plane and crossing the tarmac this time around. The other passengers had family and friends waiting for them. Sandy knew no one here and hadn't informed anyone of her arrival, so there was no one to meet her.

As she waited for her luggage to come off the plane, Sandy took a good look at where she found herself. There were no trees, no skyscrapers, no apartment building, no shopping centres, no grass and definitely few creature comforts. Regardless of how uncomfortable she felt, Sandy knew she hadn't come all this way to turn back now. She had told people that she was going to stay until she found whatever it was she was looking for, and she was totally committed to that goal. But in order to get where she wanted to go, Sandy knew she was pretty much going to be on her own for the duration.

Which was why when someone approached her, Sandy was completely caught off-guard.

"You're new to the North, aren't you?"

Startled by the voice, Sandy turned around the come face-to-face with what she could only describe as an old-timer. The man appeared to be in his late fifties, but his weather-beaten skin made him look a lot older.

"Didn't you hear me?" the man said. "Or do you not speak English?"

"I'm sorry," Sandy said as she shook herself out of her reverie. "I was surprised to hear anyone speaking to me."

"You really are new to the North, aren't you?"

"I guess it's pretty obvious, isn't it?"

The man chuckled. "Only to about every person who watched you get off the plane. We all know everyone else who came in on your flight. What you're doing here?"

"I'm sorry, I don't understand your question."

"Why are you here?"

"Oh ... I'm just visiting."

"For real?"

"Yes. Why?"

"There aren't too many people who come this far north just because they want to visit Holman," the man said. "I don't think I've heard anyone ever say that in about 10 years."

"Then I guess it's about time you heard someone say it again, isn't it?" Sandy said.

The man nodded but said nothing. As the luggage began coming into the airport building, the man spoke once more. "Name's Charlie."

Sandy stretched out her hand towards him. "Nice to meet you, Charlie. I'm Sandy."

"Where are you staying?"

"I've got a room at the hotel. I suppose there aren't too many cabs around this place."

Charlie shook his head. "As a matter of fact, there are no cabs today. But I've got room in my truck for you. I'll take you to the hotel myself."

Sandy smiled for what seemed like the first time in days. She hadn't expected to get much help from anyone on this journey, but she was glad Charlie had offered. With a considerable lack of knowledge as to where she was, Sandy was going to have to rely on the kindness of strangers. If the rest of the people she met on this journey were anything like Charlie, she was certain to reach the end.

Once her luggage had been retrieved and thrown in the back of Charlie's pickup, they began their drive into town. Nothing was said, but the ride wasn't a very long one, so there wasn't much need for small talk.

When the truck stopped, Charlie got out and pulled Sandy's bag from the back of his truck. Brushing off Sandy's insistence to carry her own bag, Charlie motioned for Sandy to go ahead and check in. Once checked in and with her room key in hand, Sandy thanked Charlie for his help.

"You've been a big help today, Charlie."

"No problem. If you need someone to show you around, just ask the desk clerk to call me. They know how to find me."

"What's your last name?"

"Why?"

"Well," Sandy said, "if I go to the desk and ask them to call Charlie, how are they going to know who you are?"

Charlie smiled. "I'm just Charlie around here. Everyone knows me, and everyone know where to find me. Besides, the day clerk is my sister."

Suddenly, Sandy came to a revelation. From the description in Jack's diary, she realized the man who had dropped her off at the hotel was the Charlie who had been such a large influence on Jack when he'd spent the summer here in Holman.

But she was too tired to broach the subject right now, and she knew there would be plenty of time. Even though she had only been in the Northwest Territories for two days, Sandy had instantly recognized that things had to be done in the own way and their own time if they were going to get done at all.

Heaving a tired sigh, Sandy picked up her suitcase and walked to a crudely lit hallway to her room. She opened the door, stepped inside the spartan room and dropped her suitcase next to the coat rack. She sat down on the small double bed and took in her new surroundings. If it was at all possible, this room was even plainer and more basic than her room in Inuvik had been.

A bed.

A two-drawer dresser.

A television.

A desk and chair.

What struck Sandy was the absolute silence in the room. She heard no cars or trucks, no sirens, as if there was no life outside as all.

She stretched out, put her head down on the pillow and looked up at the ceiling. Reaching the final leg of her journey, coming to the end of what had been an epic trip just to get here, felt somewhat anticlimactic.

Now that she had made it to Holman, Sandy had no idea what to expect next. Not wanting to fall asleep, she got up and decided to begin unpacking a bit. Throwing her suitcase onto the bed, she pulled out her clothes and the other items she had packed and tried to find logical spots for everything. Even as small as the room had seemed when she had stepped inside, Sandy found the perfect place for all her belongings.

The suitcase now dealt with, Sandy moved on to her carry-on bag. She pulled out the books she had brought and placed them on the night table next to the bed. She pulled out a bag of potato chips she had bought at the airport in Inuvik and placed it beside the television, and she put her laptop computer on the desk.

Sandy knew there was only one more item in her carry-on: Jack's diary. She carefully pulled it out of the bag and placed it at the foot of her bed. She looked around the room for a safe place to put the diary but figured the only place she would feel comfortable with it being was on the bed next to her.

As she placed it on one of the pillows on the bed, a familiar piece of paper slipped out. She recognized it as the letter that had started Sandy on this crazy adventure in the first place. Not having read it since she had left home, she found herself unfolding it and beginning to read the letter for the umpteenth time.

She laid her head on the pillow next to the diary.

Sandy,

If you're reading this letter, then you've been snooping in my office again, I've found the courage to actually give it to you or I'm not around anymore for some reason and you have to get rid of all my stuff.

I only hope to God it's not option three.

I never told you much about my life before I met you, and I guess I figured that what I did before I knew you existed wasn't nearly as exciting as the things I knew we would do after I had found you. For the most part, my life before I met you was spent going to school and playing baseball in the field behind my parents' house and cutting the neighbours' lawns for extra money. Not much that you really needed to know about, and nothing I really wanted to tell you.

But I had always planned to tell you about the summer before I met you.

That summer was probably the best time of my life—before I ran into you at that football game and spilled beer all over your best sweater, of course.

Sandy, it was the best thing that ever happened to me.

I found out who I really was, and I was able to understand my place in the world and exactly what I needed to make myself happy. I learned everything needed to know, and there was nothing else I needed. I found out what I needed to know to be a good man, an honourable man, and the kind of guy I had always hoped I would become one day. My life after that summer was never the same.

Then I met you, and the path of my life was complete. I had everything I would ever need.

I want you to read this diary and understand more about the person I was before you came into my life that sunny Saturday in late September. I want you to see the things I learned, what the summer meant to me and how it helped to shape the man I became. I want you to know the man who loves you more than life itself as you should know him—completely.

I had always planned to take you to Holman one day; you have to know that. I was just waiting for the right moment.

Hopefully, I haven't waited too long ...

I love you always.

Jack

Chapter 4

It was almost 9:00 p.m. when Sandy woke up. When her stomach began to growl, Sandy realized just how long it had been since her last meal. Hoping the kitchen was still open, she left her room and headed for the dining room.

Upon her arrival, Sandy was greeted with a warm smile.

"Hi," the woman said, "I'm Mary. You come to eat dinner?"

Sandy nodded. "If your kitchen is still open, that is."

Mary nodded her head. "We figured you'd fallen asleep right after checking in today. I told them I'd wait around for you just in case."

"How did you know I was on the flight today? I didn't see you when I checked in."

Mary smiled. "It's a small place. It didn't take long for news to spread or for people to know there's someone new in town. Take a seat, and I'll bring you a cup of coffee."

A tired smile flashed across Sandy's face before she scanned the restaurant and sat at a table in the corner. She was the only person in the restaurant, but she wanted to make sure she didn't become the centre of attention. So far the other people Sandy had met were nice enough, but she wasn't sure if everyone was going to be as welcoming. She knew that she was a total outsider; someone who came from distant part of southern Canada where people carried mobile phones and had their mail delivered to their homes, and where they could be sure to find everything and anything they needed as the grocery store or within a pretty short drive.

Mary returned with the coffee, as well as a cup for herself. When she sat down at the table, Sandy instinctively recoiled—and immediately regretted her reaction.

"I hope you don't mind," Mary said. "It's been a long day, and now that it's quiet, I think I should give my feet a rest."

"No, I don't mind at all. I just think I'm still half asleep. I must admit, it makes me a bit nervous."

"You've got no reason to be nervous. We don't bite, you know."

Sandy chuckled lightly. "I didn't mean it that way. I guess being a stranger in a place like this makes me a little bit more on guard. I know that I'm not necessarily going to be the most welcome person in town this week ..."

Mary shook her head. "Not here. You may be scared of us, but we're really not anything to be afraid of."

"I'm sorry," Sandy said. "I'm not saying things right at all. I think the trip took more out of me than I expected. This place is pretty far from home."

"This place is pretty far from everywhere else. Which of course brings me to the first question: What brings you here?"

"I'm just doing some searching."

"What for?"

"I'm searching for the thing that supposedly changed my husband's life a couple of years ago."

Mary stopped midsip. "I was following you until that point."

"My husband passed away recently," Sandy said.

"I'm sorry."

"I'm okay with it, really. When I was clearing away some of his things, I found a diary and a letter from Jack. He told me that he had spent the entire summer before we met up here, and that whatever he went through here changed his life for the better. He also said that he wanted to bring me here at some point down the road, to show me what he had seen and done and how it had changed his entire life. Unfortunately, he never got the chance to tell me about Holman before he died, so I thought I'd do it myself."

Mary got up to get the coffee pot for refills. She hadn't dared to say anything, because she figured Sandy didn't need to be pushed into telling her story and would only open up at her own pace. Mary returned to the table, filled up both her own mug and Sandy's and then sat back down.

Sandy took another sip of coffee and continued her story. "I thought I knew everything there was to know about Jack. I mean, since the very first day we met, we had shared everything with each other—or that's what I had thought."

"So why didn't he tell you about this?"

"I don't know. But the way he wrote about his experiences here is unlike anything I have read from him before. There was so much emotion and passion written into the diary entries that I almost thought I was reading someone else's diary. After I had read only the first few entries, I knew I had to come here and see the place for myself."

"Holman may seem pretty far off the beaten path, but there can be a lot of things that are only around for a short time," Mary said. "Even a couple of years. A lot can change in that much time."

Sandy took another sip of coffee. "Yeah, but I get the feeling that not much really ever changes that much around here. I figure if I'm lucky enough, I'll run into the right person or someone who knows the information I'm looking for. It will only take time."

Mary nodded, smiling. Having finished her second cup of coffee, she got up to go back to work. "I don't usually do this, but I know we've got some really nice caribou in the fridge that we haven't cooked up yet. Do you trust me enough to make you something special for your first meal in Holman?"

"I don't want to cause you too much trouble," Sandy said.

"It's no trouble. Why don't you move over to a table closer to the kitchen, and we can keep talking while I'm cooking?"

Sandy picked up her coffee cup and the coffee pot. "That sounds really nice, Mary."

Chapter 5

There's absolutely nothing to do around here when the weather is bad. Today was raining, and when I made my way over to Charlie's (after having waited more than half an hour for him to show up), I found him sitting at his kitchen table drinking coffee. He told me I had made a trip for nothing; there would be absolutely nothing going on anywhere in town today because of the rain. A day like this meant no one could work outside, no repair work could be done anywhere in town, and no one would go out fishing because if it was this miserable in Holman, the weather would be even worse out on the ocean.

All we could do was sit around, drink coffee, listen to the radio and talk about nothing in particular. After having spent two hours sitting in the kitchen talking about next to nothing, I needed to do something more constructive with my time.

When I told Charlie what I was thinking, he laughed at me. He told me I was like any other young kid he'd ever met: always looking for something to do and never content to sit back and relax. He told me he'd been the same way when he was my age, but time and experience taught him better. He then told me that he knew I couldn't help myself, but that sometime soon I would learn the truth for myself.

When we got around to leaving Charlie's house, we made it as far as the hotel, where we sat around and drank more coffee.

I sure hope the weather clears up tomorrow.

Sandy should never have had those extra few cups of coffee while chatting with Mary. After tossing and turning in her bed for the better part of an hour, she knew sleep would not be coming tonight.

Her thoughts turned to Jack, as they always did in moments of reflection like this. Having only seen a small portion of Holman on the short drive from the hotel, Sandy knew Jack would have been miserable. He had always been someone so full of energy, always looking for new and exciting ways to spend his time. In a place like this, slow and steady were the order of the day—no flashy stores, no traffic lights, not even a paved roadway.

Jack would have hated this place. That is, the Jack whom Sandy thought she knew well.

Sandy turned on the television to see if there was anything she could watch, but with only three channels to choose from, the selection was three movies Sandy had seen countless of times and had no real interest in watching again.

Her only option was to keep reading Jack's diary. She pulled it from underneath her pillow and opened it to where she had placed her bookmark.

One week down, a whole lot more to go.

I still don't know why on earth my dad thought I needed to come to this part of the country to learn something about myself. I don't know why I couldn't have just found out about myself at Pete's cottage. I think it would have been so much easier for everyone.

I have never felt so alone in my life as I do here. Making friends has never been anything too difficult for me, but in a place where you are definitely the outsider, making new friends isn't that easy. I get the feeling I'm going to have to prove myself to a whole lot of people in this town before I get any kind of respect.

The guy I'm staying with here tells me I shouldn't worry, because people around here will come around in their own time. He tells me they have seen far too many people come and go in Holman to give someone the benefit of the doubt from day one. They have done that in the past and have only ended up getting hurt when they realized they were being taken advantage of for some reason.

I guess I can't blame them for that. From what I can see, people in these parts are more than willing to give you the shirts right off their backs if you are in a bind, and I could see how they could be taken advantage of fairly easily. If they think they need to wait before I can get my respect, then I suppose I don't have much choice in the matter.

Getting used to life in a small town like this one is a hard thing, to say the least. I've never been much of a morning person, but this town doesn't really even begin to start doing anything productive until at least 11:00, if not later. And don't bother trying to get anything done on Sunday in Holman, because that simply won't happen. Nothing is open, and no one will open up for anything because Sunday is a day off.

It's ridiculous, if you ask me. I have some habits as to how I spend my weekends, and being here throws everything off completely. I can't do anything I usually do, and the only option tends to be sitting around doing nothing at all.

That's a problem for me. I don't like sitting around doing nothing, because that leaves me alone with my thoughts—and that is definitely not a good thing. There is too much angst and things I need to worry about that occupy any free moment I have, which tends to make me more edgy and nervous than I really need to be. Definitely not my idea of a fun time.

I'm young. I can't afford to be sitting around twiddling my thumbs these days. I may be stuck in a hick town, but that doesn't mean I have to give in and get bored silly.

I may never survive the summer at this rate ...

There he was. The Jack she remembered. The Jack she knew and loved. The husband she knew. The guy who could never sit still for more than 30 seconds. Sandy still missed that guy—the one that drove her around the bend because he could never sit still, even in the movie theatre. Watching his constant movement was sometimes enough to make Sandy tired.

How she missed that.

Looking at the time on the clock radio, Sandy figured the restaurant was probably open. Once her thoughts turned to a hearty breakfast and a good cup of coffee, Sandy knew it was time to get up and start the day. If today was going to be about walking around and trying to get a feel for this place, a breakfast of two eggs over easy, bacon, home fries and toast was definitely part of Sandy's plan. She showered quickly, got dressed and headed towards the restaurant.

Sandy was surprised to find she was not the only person up this early for breakfast. She was even more surprised when she recognized the other early riser.

"Good morning, Charlie."

"Well, if it isn't the newcomer. How was your first night in Holman?"

Sandy heaved a heavy sigh. "Not very restful, I'm afraid. My mind wouldn't simply stop running around in circles."

"I can understand that. I always feel that way when I'm visiting somewhere else."

"I suppose that's true. I'm just not sure how many people would find themselves here in this place, mind you. It's a long way to go to try and find yourself."

Charlie chuckled lightly. "Well, you finally managed to find yourself here, so that's the most important thing, I would imagine. Not too many people ever come to visit Holman like I told you, but those who do never forget about this place."

"Well, I intend to see as much as I can while I'm here."

Charlie didn't say anything more. He simply looked at Sandy.

The silence between Charlie and Sandy was tense, and Sandy wondered if she had said something wrong. Charlie had been her first friendly face in Holman, and she hoped she hadn't made her first mistake.

"Have you had the grand tour of Holman yet?" Charlie asked, finally breaking the silence.

"The grand tour? You make Holman sound like a big place."

Charlie chuckled once again and got up from the table. "Well, it's a pretty interesting place. But a lot of tourists never get the chance to see the things they should when they come to visit."

"Why is that?"

"Because they have the wrong tour guide."

It was Sandy's turn to chuckle. "And I suppose you're the right tour guide."

Charlie smiled and bowed. "At your service. Look, I'm pretty free today—except of course for the work I was supposed to do on the house—but if you don't mind tooling around the streets of this town with an old married guy, I'd be more than happy to show you what this place is really about. Maybe we'll even find time to visit my wife for lunch. I'll have to drop off the building supplies at some point, so she'll see I'm serious about finishing the repairs."

Sandy knew he had made her an offer she couldn't refuse. "Lead the way, Mr. Tour Guide."

Chapter 6

I've changed my mind about Charlie. He's a nutcase.

I was all set to give him the benefit of the doubt, and then he turns around and says something completely out there, totally ridiculous and 100 percent insane.

He actually asked me if I could ever see myself spending my life in a place like this. If I could live the rest of my days in Holman.

I don't know what on earth he was smoking, because I couldn't imagine anything worse than spending my entire life here. There's absolutely nothing; in many ways, you are totally cut off from the rest of the world. If I had to get out immediately, it would take me three days to get anywhere even close to being considered civilization.

Charlie learned this lesson the hard way. When his father was ill and on his deathbed, Charlie was living in Edmonton. His sister called him to come home immediately. By the time he was able to get back to Holman, his father was dead. Charlie never forgave himself for not being there to hear his father's last words.

That was the number one reason Charlie came home. Not because he missed Holman or hated living and working in Edmonton. Not because he couldn't make a living in a large city. But because he wasn't willing to sacrifice his relationship with his family in order to make more money. He'd already lost the chance to say goodbye to his father. He swore it would never happen again.

Charlie may be comfortable with the idea of coming back to this place, but coming back to somewhere like this would be admitting defeat. He says he really did try to make a go of it in the big city, but the call of his life here and the people and places he knew as a boy was too strong to ignore for long. If he ever wanted to live to be an old man, Charlie said he knew he had to come home and live out his days here.

I can't believe anyone would rather spend their days here. This place has no good restaurants. There is nowhere to buy a decent cup of coffee. I can't even buy a new pair of jeans to replace the ones I tore yesterday while helping Charlie fix his truck (which has to be older than the hills).

And everybody knows your business. It doesn't matter if you've never talked to them, because they all knew what's going on and who's doing what with whom. I don't even need to know the person; just ask the right question at the co-op, and I'll know more than I ever really wanted to know about anyone in this whole place.

I can't even call this place a town. A town would have a traffic light.

Even in her wildest dreams, Sandy had never seen another place quite like Holman. The dusty dirt roads were lined with small houses, most of which could have used a lot more than a good coat of paint to fix them up; it probably would have been easier to knock down a few of them and start from scratch. There were very few vehicles around but plenty of all-terrain vehicles and more than a few snowmobiles parked in front yards. Laundry hung out on lines and wires nailed to the sides of the houses, and the dogs quietly sat chained up to the front steps.

Probably the best-kept buildings were the church and the community centre next door. The roofs on both structures were both brand-new, the windows were all clean and the doors were painted a bright, vivid red unlike any other door Sandy had seen so far during her short tour of the town.

Sandy figured this was probably a happening place on a Sunday, and she could almost see the community celebrations going on and the kids running around outside. She was completely wrapped up in her own thoughts, and so the sound of Charlie's voice startled Sandy.

"It's so even on the snowiest day; even during the worst blizzard, you can always see it."

"I'm sorry, Charlie. What did you say?"

"I figured as much. I was talking to you about the church door, and you couldn't have been further away from here. Are you sure you're up for seeing the sights right now?"

Sandy nodded enthusiastically. She didn't want to have to sit around and talk anymore with Charlie, because the anxious feeling in the pit of her stomach told her that pretty soon she'd have to tell him more about Jack.

As Charlie pointed out the many sights not found on a tourist map, Sandy began to wonder about her tour guide. She knew Charlie had been born and raised here, but still she couldn't understand what made him stay here. She had read Jack's words, but she had yet to hear any kind of explanation from Charlie. She had asked him questions from time to time, but Charlie never really revealed any information about himself. Sandy wondered if he was keeping secrets from her for some strange reason.

For his part, Charlie was not comfortable talking about himself with someone he hardly knew. Everyone in Holman knew all there was to know about Charlie, and that suited him just fine. Sandy was a different story, because he sensed that the more they spent time together, the more they would have to start talking about feelings—which he did not think would be easy for either of them.

They drove along in silence for a while, both lost in their own thoughts and insecurities. Neither was willing to strike up the conversation because they were afraid to find out where talking would take them. Keeping quiet had always been a safer choice for both Charlie and Sandy, and they were quite happy to fall back into old habits and enjoy the ride.

After another 20 minutes, Charlie pulled the truck over at the side of a hill. "I need a smoke break, Sandy. That, and to stretch my legs a little bit. I actually promised my wife I would stop in a check up on a friend who lives in that house just over there, and I thought I should do it before I forget."

"Sounds like a good idea. Take your time."

Charlie nodded. "I'll meet you back here in 10 minutes."

He fumbled around in his pockets for his lighter as he walked away. Sandy didn't really know where she was going, but something told her to climb the hill and enjoy the view. It was an easy climb, and she was more than richly rewarded for her efforts, because from the top of the hill, she could see the entire community.

Never had she felt such a feeling of peace and serenity. In the weeks since Jack's funeral, there had been a pain in her heart that wouldn't leave Sandy alone. She knew it had to be grief, and she had expected as much— but she had never expected the physical pain that came along with the feelings. Her insides craved just one more minute with Jack, and in many ways being here made that craving even worse.

Having a moment alone, Sandy reached into her bag and pulled out the diary. As she ran her fingers over its cover, she began talking to Jack, as if he was right there beside her. "I think you know how much I miss you, and I'm doing my best to go on without you. I had come here to see this place for myself, because if I had stayed in our house one more minute, I never would have survived. I'm not leaving until I find my answers, Jack. I can't. But you of all people should know that. I only hope I'm not sorry I went looking for answers in the first place."

Sandy flipped through the diary to find the next entry.

Chapter 7

It's funny. I thought I would be completely miserable without all the amenities of home this summer. In fact, I thought I'd never be able to survive one day without a few of them.

How wrong I was.

I have learned I don't need those fancy gadgets to get through the day. Now, I realize how wrong I really was. There is very little in the way of creature comforts I need in order to actually survive.

Watching the people here go through their daily lives without a lot of the things I thought were essential proves you don't need much to live a good life.

I know more than one person in this place who doesn't even have a telephone. I can't imagine not having a phone, but those who don't seem to be too worried, and they aren't even out of touch with friends or family simply because they can't call them on a regular basis.

There are people who have never—and I mean never—locked their doors. From where I stand, that is an invitation for some serious theft or property damage, or something even worse.

Here, people don't even have to knock upon entering your house, because every guest is always a welcome guest. Your house is open to friends and family, and even to people who are just visiting Holman for work purposes.

I think it's crazy, but they seem to enjoy their lives so much more than the people I know, simply because they know they live somewhere safe and their neighbours are always looking out for them.

I think that would be a nice feeling.

When Charlie had finished his cigarette and returned to the truck, he saw Sandy sitting on the hill. Even from the bottom of the hill, he could tell she was crying. Charlie decided he needed to give Sandy some kind of distraction.

He climbed the hill quietly and then cleared his throat. "I hope you're feeling strong, Sandy."

"Pardon me?"

Charlie chuckled. "I've got a lot of lumber waiting for me at the co-op, and there is a bunch of other stuff I need to finish the addition to my house. I'm going to need a lot of help getting them into the back of my truck."

"Well, I might not be as strong as you are," Sandy said. "But I think it's only fair that I give you as much help loading up your truck as I can."

"That's exactly the answer I wanted to hear from you. Let's go."

The two jumped into the truck and drove to the co-op in silence. As Charlie pulled up in front of the red wooden building, Sandy noticed that his pickup was in fact the only vehicle outside. The rest of the front area was filled with all-terrain vehicles big and small, new and old.

Charlie turned off the engine and turned to face Sandy. "Are you ready to see the inside of a real-life, honest-to-goodness Arctic store?"

Sandy nodded. "Absolutely."

The two jumped out of the old pickup and headed for the front door. Charlie opened the door and let Sandy enter the co-op first.

What she saw was certainly not what she had expected to find at all. In her own imagination, Sandy had thought the store would just look like any other store she had ever been in before now. But what she found was a place full of everything one could possibly need, and a whole lot more. There were countless bins of nails and screws hanging on the walls, right next to a vast selection of tools. In one corner was an old soda machine that took nothing higher than quarters. In another corner was the electronics area (she couldn't call it a section), which consisted of a television and a DVD player. Between the two corners, chest freezers were filled with a wide range of food and a lot of items Sandy got fresh at her corner store. Sandy figured that some of these items had flown up on the very same flight that had brought her to Holman.

"Look here, fellas. It's that lady looking for her northern experience," Sandy heard from behind her.

When she turned around, Sandy saw a grey-haired man with weather-beaten skin wearing an old blue jean jacket and an Esso baseball cap. She immediately recognized him as someone she had seen hanging around the airport building the day she'd arrived.

"Cool it, Peter, "Charlie said as he stepped in behind Sandy. "We're just here to pick up my delivery. Sandy doesn't need to deal with you right now."

"And why not?" Peter asked as he stepped closer to Sandy, staring her down. "I should think that if she really wants to get to know Holman, she should see it all—the good, the bad, and the ugly."

"She's going to see it all, Peter. Trust me."

Charlie's words of reassurance served to further inflame Peter's sense of outrage. As one of the employees at the co-op, Peter had seen more than his share of people come and go, and a lot of the visitors who passed through the doors of his store had no real interest in learning anything about Holman because their only goal was to try to find something worth taking home to show their friends and prove that they had actually been here. From what he could see, Sandy was just that kind of person.

"If I know you, Charlie, you're going to show her all the pretty parts of this place and ignore all the bad things—things that are the way they are because people from the south don't understand what it's really like to live up here." He turned to Sandy. "Why on earth did a woman like you decide to come up to Holman?"

Somewhat taken aback by Peter's attitude, Sandy tried to square up her shoulders in order to look more confident. She was terrified inside, but she did not want to give Peter any reason to think she was nothing more than "another person from the south."

"I'm here because I want to find out what my husband found here," Sandy said firmly.

"So you're not even here to see the real Holman, are you?"

"No ... I mean yes."

Peter looked at Charlie and smiled smugly. "See? Didn't I tell you about her? She's just here on some silly quest to find herself, and she has convinced herself that coming here is the answer. The truth is, lady, this place isn't some holiday destination. This is my home, and Charlie's home, and I am sick and tired of people coming up here for only a short time and then going back to their nice, comfortable lives and telling everyone they've lived in the Arctic and are experts on the subject when that couldn't be further from the truth."

Sensing Sandy's imminent collapse, Charlie stepped in between her and Peter. "That's enough, Peter. Sandy and I are here to pick up my delivery. Why don't you go get it ready, and I'll drive around back so we can load up my truck and go about our business?"

Still grumbling, Peter headed for the back of the store.

Charlie said, "I'm sorry about him, Sandy. He's been a bit of a grump since his son moved to Yellowknife for a job. Let's get my supplies and get out of here."

Chapter 8

Maybe there are some good points about living in a place like this—not many, but at least one or two. For example, there is very little concern with the petty things that have become obsessions for many people back home. There is very little self-interest to be found in these people, probably because it is pretty much them against nature around here, and if one person gets lost on the land or someone gets killed in a freak accident, there is a good chance that everyone knew the person or had some kind of history with them.

The fishing is the best I have ever seen. Charlie took me out to his favourite fishing spot yesterday, and I don't think there has been a day I enjoyed more. We spent the entire day out there, casting out lines and pulling in the Arctic charr like the ocean was full of fish. He'd even snuck a few beers into the boat before we took off from the house, and we spent the day chatting, laughing and fishing.

I can't say I'd want to live my life here, but I can see what it is about Holman that Charlie likes so much. From what I can tell, he is happy with this life and what he's got going, so I can't really fault him for that.

Maybe I'll be lucky enough to find my life and be as happy as Charlie seems to be.

"Stop thinking."

Once again, Charlie's insightful comments caught Sandy off guard.

"How do you do that?" she asked.

"What?"

"Know when I'm thinking too hard."

Charlie chuckled. "I was actually only guessing. What could possibly be that important to keep you so distracted?"

"It's nothing," Sandy said.

"You're still thinking about what Peter said to you, aren't you?"

Sandy didn't answer. When the silence continued for a couple of minutes more, Charlie knew he had hit the nail on the head. He would admit to himself that he had the same reservations about Sandy and her real reason for coming to Holman at first, but he had come to realize her reasons for this journey were more complex than anyone could understand, even if she spent the rest of her life here.

He knew she was here out of love. Sandy had not come out and said it, but the look on her face as Sandy spoke of his old friend made him miss Jack even more. He also knew that he was going to have to explain himself to Sandy sooner or later, but for right now he was going to let Sandy find her way first.

"I'm really sorry about what he said, Sandy. It's just that some people don't appreciate strangers coming to Holman who claim to be visiting."

"Why? What is it about me he didn't like?"

Charlie shook his head. "It's not you. Peter and I have lived here long enough to have seen a lot of people breeze through here claiming to have buckets of money to help us out, but when all is said and done, they have only made us promises because it suits them at the time. They get what they want or need from us, and then they get the promotion they have been working for, or they find somewhere more exciting to work. We end up with the short end of the stick. They go back to wherever it is they came from and claim to be experts on the north, but they haven't a clue."

"Is that what people think of me?" Sandy asked, stunned. "Do they think I'm here to take something away?"

"Not everyone feels that way, Sandy. I can't say Peter is the only one, but I can tell you the majority of people in Holman will be more than willing to help you out. I was hoping it wasn't going to happen yet, but I knew that sooner or later you'd run into someone who would tell you his or her opinion, and it wouldn't be positive."

"What about you?" Sandy asked.

"Me? I'm not worth that much thought," Charlie replied. "Trust me."

"I don't know about that. From what I can see, I'll bet you have all kinds of fascinating stories about yourself."

"Everyone thinks other people's lives are considerably more fascinating than his own," he said. "I mean, I think your story is pretty interesting."

"But I haven't really told you a lot about myself," Sandy said.

"It doesn't matter. What you have neglected to say is far more informative than what you have said to me."

Sandy didn't have a witty comeback for Charlie's comment. She simply stared at him wondering what he meant by his remarks, suddenly self-conscious about her choice of words. She had always thought of herself as a relatively private person, yet this stranger seemed to have a direct line into her very soul.

"You don't feel like Peter, do you?" Sandy asked him.

"What do you mean? Do I think your reasons for being here aren't about really getting to know Holman?"

"You said he wasn't the only person who felt that way about me. Are you trying to tell me you feel the same way, but you somehow feel responsible for me, so you're just being nice?"

"What the hell are you talking about?" Charlie said, clearly insulted by Sandy's sudden attack. "I have gone out of my way to try to make you feel more welcome here, and you dare to insult me like that? I have a lot of better things to do with my time, Sandy. I don't need to be playing tour guide to a southerner who wouldn't last a day in this place if I hadn't offered to help. Come to think of it, you'd probably still be sitting at the airport if I hadn't offered you a ride to the hotel!"

Sandy instantly felt ashamed of her insinuations. She knew Charlie was trying to help her out, but Peter's comments had brought up one of her biggest insecurities about this entire trip. She knew she was coming to strange place, and she knew there would be people who would not be welcoming. Sandy had worried that no one would bother to help her out.

She sighed heavily. "I'm sorry, Charlie. I shouldn't have said that."

"You're damn right, you shouldn't have said that! I'm doing more for you than I need to!"

"You're right. I'm sorry. I'm just afraid."

Sandy's last comment began to soften Charlie's temper. "What are you talking about?"

She hopped up on to the tailgate of the pickup truck. "I was afraid I'd get here and no one would want to help me. I'd heard the stories of how hard life in the Arctic can be, and I guess I projected feelings of bitterness upon everyone here. When Peter came out and said the things I'd been waiting to hear, I reacted in kind to everyone else. I'm sorry, Charlie. Please."

Charlie's sigh was music to Sandy's ears. "It's all right. I should apologize to you too. I guess Peter's words hit me harder than I expected them to, and I took it out on you. He really is nothing more than an old grouch, and I don't want you to think everyone in Holman feels the way he does."

"So people *do* feel I'm intruding? I've only been here one day!"

"I told you that a lot of people in Holman have been lied to by people who came up from the south and promised to help, myself included. Almost every year, some new face breezes in and claims to have the answers to all of our problems. Once they have managed to convince us that the plan is going ahead, they go home, and we never see or hear from them again. Holman has seen its share of good times and bad times, and some people have learned not to trust people they don't know because all that brings is more heartache if they buy into whatever they are selling."

"I'm sorry, Charlie. I shouldn't have said what I did. It's because I'm starting to be afraid that I will never find the answers I have come looking for."

"I can't promise you the answers, Sandy, but I can promise you I'll do whatever I can do to help,."

Sandy hopped off the tailgate and put a hand on Charlie's shoulder.

"Thanks, Charlie. I feel better already."

Chapter 9

I'm in trouble.

I think I'm starting to enjoy myself here. That can only mean I'm starting to like my summer in the middle of nowhere.

Up until now, I thought that would have been absolutely impossible. I was dead set against spending my summer here, and I was determined to hate every single thing about this place before I arrived. I didn't expect to find any reason to enjoy myself, and I figured I'd never come close to fitting in.

But little by little, I've started to strip my life down to its barest necessities. I've realized that there's more to do on a Friday night than to go downtown and catch the latest movie. I've realized that there are more types of music I might listen to on my own, without someone pointing a gun to my head. I've learned there are people who might not be well-educated in terms of a proper education, but they know far more than I will ever learn in my lifetime.

I see that there's more to life than what I had thought my life should be. I realize that the important thing is not how change will affect me, but how to deal with change, learn to accept whatever changes and move on. Back home, everyone is more concerned about how the changes will force them to make changes in their own lives; here in Holman, even the smallest change can cause a considerable amount of change within the community. Every new technological introduction endangers the traditional way of life that has been practiced for hundreds of years by making it impossible for the youth to continue the ways of their ancestors.

Although there is great change happening on almost a daily basis, the young people and the young at heart recognize that the practices of the past must be safeguarded. In order to fully understand what those who came before had to endure in order to simply survive, the traditions of the past must still be practiced today. That's why a lot of houses have microwave ovens, yet the women still know how to make bannock over an open fire. It's why people have all-terrain vehicles but can still find their way on the land, travelling by dog team.

I know a lot, and I'm pretty self-sufficient. But compared to these people, I'm a novice.

Lunch brought Sandy and Charlie back to town and to the hotel restaurant once more. Although it was the only restaurant in town, Sandy also knew it was probably the best place to grab a cup of coffee and pick up the latest news and goings-on. She also enjoyed the silence and not being forced to talk about anything, because she wasn't up for small talk at the moment.

For his part, Charlie needed to poke around a bit more to know if he was still doing the right thing. As he picked up the creamer and fixed up yet another cup of coffee, he knew they had been quiet long enough. "Tell me how you met Jack."

"What?"

"We've been sitting here for 30 minutes, and you haven't said a single word. That tells me you have something pretty heavy on your mind. And I'd bet my next pay cheque on it having something to do with your husband."

Sandy smiled sadly at Charlie's assessment. She realized just how well people in Holman could read her emotions, and they weren't afraid to call her on her behaviour. She had found it somewhat disconcerting at first, but she was beginning to find great comfort in knowing she was really understood.

"We met at a football game," Sandy said as she got up to refill her coffee cup. "Which is odd in itself, because I have never been to another football game since."

"So you're not a football fan anymore?"

Sandy chuckled. "I never was."

Charlie looked puzzled. "You've lost me."

She leaned against the counter. "The only reason I went was because my friends would not take no for an answer. My friend Alison had a crush on the kicker and hoped that if he saw her at the game, he might want to chat with her. "I was never much of a sports fan growing up, so it wasn't really my thing. I had fun spending time with my friends, but I was really bored.

"Then at one point, I needed to use the washroom, and ..."

Sandy's eyes glazed over. As if almost in a trance, she sat down and didn't say another word. She took a couple of sips of her coffee.

It was then Charlie saw the tears begin to well up in her eyes. "You met Jack," he said, trying to move the conversation forward.

"More like we ran into each other. He was on his way back to his seat after a stop at the concession stand for a few beers for himself and his friends."

Mary walked back into the dining room for her lunch break and pulled out the chair next to Charlie to sit down. "Don't tell me you got in between a man and his beer, Sandy. That is an offence punishable by death in some places," she said sarcastically, having heard the last portion of Sandy's story.

Sandy said, "It was even worse than that, I'm afraid. When I ran into him, he proceeded to spill the beers all over my dress and the front of his jeans. When I looked up at the man who had ruined my favourite dress, I saw the most beautiful boy I had ever seen."

Again Sandy's thoughts drifted back to that day, and she was silent again. *Ice-blue eyes. Long, wavy brown hair. Soft, boyish features. A beautiful smile ...*

Mary smiled brightly. "Sounds like you weren't too angry about the dress when you saw who had spilled beer all over it."

Sandy shook her head. "No. He was genuinely sorry, much more concerned about me and my dress than he was about the 20 dollars in beer he had just wasted—or the massive wet spot on the front of his jeans. He was so cute as he helped me sop up the beer on my dress while still trying to be gentlemanly about it."

There was another pause in the conversation as Sandy lost herself in her thoughts once more. This time, Charlie decided not to interrupt. As much as he wanted to hear more about how his friend had met the woman sitting in front of him, Charlie was painfully aware of the fact that Sandy was still grieving the loss of her husband. He knew that as with any loss, time was the only thing that could help.

Oddly enough, Charlie welcomed the silence. While Sandy was thinking about her first meeting with Jack, he was doing the very same thing.

He remembered a scrawny, selfish boy who grumpily stomped off the plane and slumped himself into the passenger seat of an old pickup truck. Jack's father had warned Charlie that Jack was not looking forward to spending his summer in Holman, so helping him to learn anything about life was going to be a challenge.

But as grumpy and miserable as Jack was on the short ride back to Charlie's house (where Jack was going to stay for the summer), Charlie saw something in his new charge that gave him hope. Jack was really looking at things, not simply letting the scenery pass him by.

Jack finally began to soften as the truck reached the house and he was introduced to Janet and then Alice, Charlie's 17-year-old daughter. It was then that Charlie saw that Jack was someone worth getting to know.

His own reverie was interrupted by the sound of Sandy's voice. She said, "I'm sorry, Charlie. I drifted off on my own again."

"Don't worry about it," Mary said. "Charlie's been doing the same thing."

Sandy chuckled, clearly embarrassed. "I really am sorry. Where was I?"

"You had just looked up to see the most beautiful boy you had ever seen."

"Right. He was trying to clean up the beer on my dress, but it wasn't working."

"So what happened next?"

"Jack gave me his sweater—and his phone number."

"His phone number?"

"It was only to make sure he got his sweater back," Sandy said, trying to stifle a chuckle.

"Right. Of course," Mary said with a wink and wry smile. "You're a beautiful girl. Like he wasn't hoping for more than his sweater back."

The smile that crossed Sandy's face showed both Charlie and Mary that she knew exactly what Jack had been hoping would happen. "Be that as it may, Jack gave me his sweater. I put it on and went back to my friends."

"And what did your friends say when you returned wearing a stranger's sweater?"

"They asked me where I got it. So I told them. A few days later, I called Jack back so I could arrange to give him back his sweater. We spent nearly two hours talking about anything and everything. Twenty minutes after I hung up the phone, Jack was knocking on my dorm room, door looking for his sweater. That was the last day I spent without him, until …"

Sandy's silence spoke volumes. Mary wiped a tear away from her cheek, and Charlie sat in stunned silence.

After a few minutes, Sandy pulled herself together slightly and stood up. "I think I need to be alone for a while."

Charlie replied, "Whatever you think is best, Sandy. You know where to find us if you want to come back to the house."

As Sandy left the dining room, Mary stood up to get the coffee pot and refilled her and Charlie's cups. "You know, you are going to have to tell her the truth soon," she noted.

"What do you mean?"

"You know damn well what I mean, big brother

"It's not that easy to slip that detail into pleasant conversation, Mary."

"I don't care. If she finds out from someone else, it will be ugly. You know that as well as I do."

Charlie nodded. He knew his sister wasn't telling him anything he didn't already know, but that didn't make the reality any easier to face. He knew keeping the truth hidden was not the answer, but it didn't mean he was ready to tell Sandy.

"She's not going to understand, Mary. She's going to be so angry."

"Yes. she probably will be angry at first. She might not even want to see you for a few days. But she'll get over it. The woman who sat here, poured out her heart and got lost in her memories of her dead husband doesn't strike me as one to hold a grudge."

Mary was right, and Charlie knew as much. Sandy would ultimately forgive him for keeping secrets, but the idea of breaking Sandy's heart and disappointing her was more than he wanted to think about.

The truth was, Charlie had also been grieving the loss of a good friend. Even though Jack's first days in Holman were difficult for everyone, once the dust settled, their time together was wonderful for both men. When it came time for Jack to go back to his life, Charlie knew their friendship would never end, until death.

Charlie had secretly always hoped he would see Jack again, but it wasn't until he realized that Sandy was Jack's wife that he knew how deep his loss had been.

"You don't understand, Mary. You can't understand what this would mean."

"Telling Sandy the truth—that you knew her husband and loved him like a brother? How do I not understand that? You are my brother. I have known you and loved and worshipped the ground you walk on my entire life. I know what Jack meant to you, and I have kept my mouth shut because I realized it was up to you to tell that woman the truth when you were good and ready. But I do not understand for the life of me why you are not willing to tell her that you knew Jack. She has come a very long way to find answers, and she doesn't even realize the one person she trusts the most on this entire island is the one person who has the answers she is looking for—and those answers she doesn't even realizes she needs to get."

Charlie shook his head furiously. He couldn't do it. He simply couldn't tell Sandy the truth.

For her part, Mary was flabbergasted. Her brother had never backed away from the truth in his life, but she could see the fear in his eyes when he thought of admitting this one little secret to Sandy. It made absolutely no sense.

Then suddenly the answer dawned on her. She reached over to place her hand on Charlie's left forearm. "Wait a minute—I get it. This has nothing to do with the fact you have been lying to Sandy."

"What? What do you mean?"

"The reason you don't want to tell Sandy that you knew Jack has nothing to do with Sandy or Jack. This has to do with Alice."

"If I talk to Sandy about Jack, I am going to have to talk about Alice. You know as well as I do that Jack and Alice were inseparable the entire time he was here. How do I explain that to Jack's wife?"

Mary knew Charlie rarely talked about Alice, his only daughter, who had been dead three years now. A terrible boating accident took her before her time and left Charlie with the biggest whole in his heart.

Jack and Alice had been very close while he was here, primarily because Alice had been the first friend he had made when he got to Holman. Mary had always thought they had been more than just friends while Jack was in town, but it wasn't until he had returned home that she found out how close they had been during that summer.

"I know you still miss Alice, but even she would want you to tell Sandy the truth about Jack's summer here."

Charlie looked despondent. "But that would mean I have to open up that wound again. Mary, I'm not sure I am strong enough to patch it back up again."

"You seem to think you're in this alone, my brother. If you tell Sandy the truth, that means I am going to have to tell her the truth too. She's going to be hurt and angry, but if you, Janet, and I are here to help support her, she'll get through this just fine. Besides, you know damn well that if Alice were still here, she would want you to do everything in your power to make sure Sandy knew the truth—all of it."

Charlie nodded. "I know you're right. I know it. It doesn't make it any easier."

Chapter 10

As I sat off in the corner last night at the community feast, I finally admitted to myself that I will miss this place once I leave. I knew early on this would turn out to be a summer I would never forget, but I thought I would think of it as the most horrible summer of my life.

Now I know it has been an experience of a lifetime. I have learned more about myself than I ever thought there was to know about myself, and I am lucky to have reached this point at such an early age. I have my entire life ahead of me, and I know I will be able to face the ups and downs while remaining centred and grounded. That may sound trite for me to say at this point in my life, but I truly believe it. Even as the words flow from my pen and appear on the paper, I know these are my true thoughts.

While standing off in the corner as an observer of all that was going on around me, I was relaxed. I didn't feel the need to make my presence felt, simple because I knew that if someone wanted to talk to me, they knew I was standing over in the corner, and they would come over of their own accord to strike up a conversation. It wasn't about me at an event like that, because the feast was for everyone. It was the chance for the people to get together and share a meal, a couple of stories and a whole lot of laughter. More often than not, someone has brought along a guitar or fiddle and managed to convince someone to start singing the old-time country favourites, or even a traditional gospel tune or two. If we're really lucky, the singing turns to dancing, and the night turns into early morning.

I don't even like to dance. I'm a terrible dancer. My parents have always told me I had two left feet. Here in Holman, there are only two types of dancing: jigging and drum dancing, both of which require a great deal of talent and ability to perform. But my new friends never take no for an answer, and before I knew it, I was up on the dance floor giving it my best shot. Once the dancing was over, everyone knew exactly why I had been hiding in the corner.

I had made a fool of myself, but I wasn't all that embarrassed. I had fun, I enjoyed myself, and what could have been a huge disaster for me turned out to be a good time. I think I just lucked out, if you ask me.

"You're not supposed to be standing here, Sandy. The fun is taking place over there."

Sandy turned around to find Mary walking up behind her with a few other people in town. She didn't know anyone of the others, but she recognized the faces. "I know I'm not in the right place, Mary. I just wanted to watch from the sidelines for a while," Sandy said.

"You can't fool me. I can tell you were thinking about your husband.'

Sandy was surprised. She didn't think she was that transparent, but if Mary could tell what she was thinking, perhaps she wasn't hiding it as well as she thought. "Am I that obvious, Mary? I was hoping I was hiding my emotions a little better than that."

"It's your eyes," said one of the other women. "If what Mary says is right, then your husband was well-loved when he was alive."

"Sandy, this is my sister Sarah. She's here from Inuvik for the weekend."

"I know I've seen your face somewhere before, but I can't pinpoint exactly where I would have seen you in Inuvik," Sandy said apologetically.

"I work at the front desk of the hotel you stayed at in town," Sarah said. "And I don't blame you for not remembering. Coming up here for the first time can be extremely overwhelming. A lot of people have felt the same way. How are you enjoying your stay here in Holman?"

"I'm really enjoying myself here," Sandy said. "Charlie and Janet and all the other people I've met have been very friendly, so it hasn't been too hard to get settled here."

Another woman chuckled. "If you're having an easy time getting settled here, you're stronger than a lot of other people who've visited," she said, extending her hand towards Sandy. "I'm Jane. It's nice to meet you."

Sandy shook her hand and nodded her head. "It's nice to meet you too. Up to now, the only women I've met have been Mary and Janet, so having the chance to put names to a few more faces is most definitely welcome."

"Now that the introductions are almost over, why don't we go join the rest of the people? It's not much fun standing here and watching the world go by."

Still somewhat unsure of her desire to really get involved in the celebration, Sandy reluctantly followed the other women towards the action. She spent most of the afternoon lagging behind the group, but she had to admit she did enjoy herself, even if she was somewhat melancholy. She managed to chuckle once or twice when the others told a joke, but her heart wasn't into being in a good mood, because her heart was with Jack.

When the fun was finally over and it was time to go home, Charlie, Janet, and Sandy piled back into the truck and headed for home.

"I understand why you drove today, Charlie," Sandy said. "I'm so tired I think I have the energy to crawl into bed and not much else."

"I'm an old pro at these events, Sandy. I know how exhausting they can be."

"I'm not sure I'll ever doubt you again, Charlie."

Janet laughed. "Don't say stuff like that to him, Sandy. He'll never let you live it down."

Charlie said, "I'm not that bad, Janet. Besides, a little stroking of the ego is never a bad thing."

"Is that all you need stroked today? "Janet said suggestively, waggling her eyebrows.

"Not in front of your company, Janet," Charlie said.

Sandy shook her head. "It's all right, Charlie. I can't expect you to act like you don't love each other because I'm grieving for my own loss. In fact, I could probably get a room at the hotel for tonight, if you'd like."

"You'll do nothing of the kind," Charlie said defiantly. "You are going to come back and stay with us in our house tonight, as usual, and there will be no discussion of moving tonight or any other night, regardless of what Janet and I might get up to."

Janet said, "I did notice you were a little sad today, Sandy. Are you okay?"

Sandy shook her head. "No, but I'll get through it. I'm just missing Jack something awful today. He would have loved an event like that."

Not wanting to make Sandy feel any worse, neither Charlie nor Janet said anything further for the rest of the ride home. When the three got out and headed inside, Charlie asked Sandy one final question.

"Are you sure you're going to be okay?"

Sandy smiled and then gave Charlie a quick peck on the cheek. "I'm not quite sure, but I appreciate being asked. I think I'm going to turn in early tonight, so I'll leave you two young lovebirds alone in peace and quiet. And if you do decide to get up to anything, I'll just put the pillow over my ears and pretend I don't hear anything."

Leaving Charlie and Janet in embarrassed laughter, Sandy headed for her room and closed the door behind her. Without getting undressed, Sandy climbed into bed and pulled Jack's diary from underneath the pillow, clutching it close to her chest before dissolving into tears.

Chapter 11

Finally a chance for a quick cup of coffee.

I can't remember the last time I worked this hard. Charlie works harder than I thought was humanly possible—and he's got almost 20 years on me. But I suppose if I had been doing this much work every single day since I was a kid, I'd probably feel the same way.

Working with Charlie is quite the experience, let me tell you. He works hard, but there never seems to be any rush to get the job done. The work always gets done in the long run, but there is no pressure to get things done quickly. In the long run, I think things are done right the first time.

Before now, I have always looked for the shortcut in whatever I was doing. I may not have always done a good job, but the job got done, and that was what mattered. Where I come from, the most important thing is getting everything accomplished in as little time as possible, because there are always 15 other things left to be done by the end of the day. It never seemed to matter if the job had been done poorly, because it could always be redone at some point in the future.

Now I'm not so sure. I think part of the reason people do things properly the first time here is because it's not as simple to get the tools and equipment you need for the job. I mean, when the co-op has only a limited amount of space and inventory, you only have a limited amount of whatever it is you're trying to get your hands on. Now throw into the mix the fact that shipments didn't come in on a regular basis, and you make sure the job gets done right the very first time.

That's a good way to go through life, I think. I have been watching Charlie do everything with a great attention to detail no matter what the task was, from cleaning the toilet to building a house. And it's not that Charlie is a perfectionist, because it's quite obvious perfection is not his life strategy; he simply does things the way they should be done.

Not a bad way to go through life, if you ask me.

Walking through Holman and lost in her thoughts, Sandy took some comfort in the peace and solace that came from every part of town. Without the noise and bother of the larger cities that served as a backdrop to Sandy in her daily life back home, the only thing she was left with here was her own inner voice, forcing her to take a hard look at the path she had now followed.

And for today, her path led her to the hotel. Realizing she hadn't eaten all day, Sandy decided to drop in for a bite and catch up on all the gossip with Mary. She'd been so busy in the last couple of days that she hadn't been able to see Mary for her regular afternoon cup of coffee, and Sandy was surprised to find she missed the daily ritual. when she walked through the door and walked towards Mary, Sandy knew she was not the only one who had missed the chance to talk.

"Hi, Sandy," Mary said with a smile. "I was just thinking there was a pot of coffee sitting in the dining room with your name on it."

Sandy chuckled, relieved by the way she was greeted. In a very short time, Mary had become quite an important person to Sandy. If the visitors were lucky, they were able to make some great connections with the people of Holman, and Sandy knew she could consider herself very lucky to have been accepted so fully. Sandy also knew that when she finally left Holman to return to her life, Mary would be one of the people with whom she would always remember.

As Sandy sat down at a table, Mary brought two clean cups and the coffee pot over to join her. "I just made this pot 15 minutes ago," Mary said. "I even pulled out that flavoured coffee that I knew you like. Something in the back of my mind told me you might be in today."

"I'm sorry I haven't been spending a lot of time with you recently. I've been hanging out with Charlie and Janet, and I have been seeing a lot of

Holman from the perspective of a long-time resident rather than from my big-city perspective."

"I know, and it's okay. If I were spending all my time in a new place like you are, I'd probably not have much time to stop for coffee either."

"It's not like I've been doing it on purpose. I just find I am having a problem telling time here, even if I am wearing a watch."

"No one spends a lot of time looking at their watches here, Sandy," Mary said, taking another sip of her coffee. "It's not because we don't wear watches or want to know what time it is, it's because time passes on a completely different system here. Things happen when they happen, and no one ever seems to be worried when something happens later than expected."

Sandy was listening to Mary, but her mind was still on Jack and his birthday. She missed him almost every day of her life, but the pain and loneliness was magnified this day. Try as she might to move the memories to the back of her mind, all that she could think of was her husband.

"You're not even listening to me anymore, are you?"

Sandy snapped back to reality upon hearing Mary's last statement, and she knew she had been caught. Sandy smiled sheepishly and shrugged her shoulders. "I'm sorry. My mind is somewhere else today."

"You feel like sharing?"

Sandy remained silent for a few minutes and bowed her head, almost trying to will the tears not to start falling. When she accepted that she was fighting a losing battle, Sandy looked back up at Mary with the tears welling up in her eyes. "It's Jack's birthday."

Without saying a word, Mary moved over to sit next to Sandy and wrapped her arms around her. The warmth of Mary's embrace made Sandy comfortable enough to let the tears fall freely, allowing the memories to wash over her and work to heal some part of the hole in her heart. For one small minute, Sandy felt a little better.

She pulled back from Mary's embrace, smiling weakly. "Thanks, I needed that a bit."

"You know, talking about Jack might help you a little," Mary said tentatively, not really sure how Sandy would react to her asking for more of the story. "Tell me what happened to Jack."

Sandy took a deep breath. Her eyes seemed as if they were trying to look at something off in the distance, and Sandy started her story. "He was taking the afternoon off. I'd just been told I'd got the promotion I was up for, and I called him to see if he could take the afternoon off so we could have a little celebration. We'd both been working really hard, and I figured it was about time we took some time for ourselves.

"He was so proud of me. Jack knew how hard I'd been working for the both of us, and he always told me that no one deserved to get that promotion more than I did. He was so very happy for me, for us. He said he was going to stop and get a few things before he came home, and then we'd celebrate. I knew he was going out to buy me a gift, but I didn't want anything. I just wanted him to come home."

As the memories began to get more painful and closer to the surface, Sandy felt the need to get up and move, almost as if it was the only way she would survive telling the story—to keep moving forward. She stood up and walked away from Mary and the table, turning completely so as not to see the emotion play across Mary's face

"I waited for Jack for two hours. When he still wasn't home, I got worried. Just as I was going to start making phone calls to try to find him, the police knocked at my door. They told me it was a drunk driver. He went through a red light, and Jack never saw him coming. The officers at the door told me he was killed instantly.

"They say no one should live long enough to see their children buried," Sandy said. "But the people who say that have got it so wrong. No one should live long enough to see their spouse buried, and you sure as hell shouldn't be a widow by the time you hit thirty."

Snapping back to the present once again, Sandy took a deep breath, wiped her face, and sat back down at the table. She was completely exhausted, and Mary gave her a few minutes to compose herself. "I'm sorry, Mary. You don't need me falling to pieces in your restaurant."

Mary shook her head. "You don't need to apologize for anything. I know how it goes when you lose someone you love, even a husband."

Sandy was startled by Mary's words. Although they had spent a great deal of time talking, most of the conversation had been monopolized by Sandy's problems. She wasn't someone who always had to be the centre of attention, but she had been ignorant of what the other people around her might have been feeling in the wake of her own heartache.

"You lost a husband too?" Sandy whispered gently. "My God, Mary, you must think I'm a horrible person, with the way I've been going on and on about Jack."

"Not at all. I know what it feels like, as if you're the only person in the world who feels as much pain as you do now. You feel like the heart in your chest will never beat again, and that there is no one who truly understands the depth of your pain, and there's absolutely no one else in the entire universe who will be as heartbroken as you are now."

Sandy nodded. "You're not too far off the mark."

Mary smiled and placed a hand on Sandy's. "It's a terrible pain, I know. I wouldn't wish that kind of pain on my worst enemy. All I can tell you—and you probably won't believe me—is that things will get better with time. How much time it will take, I can't tell you, but it will happen."

Sandy took another sip of coffee. Mary picked up the coffee pot and refilled both hers and Sandy's cup; she knew this conversation wasn't over. She hadn't planned to go into her own personal history now, but Mary knew she was going to have no choice but to reveal her own heartbreak if Sandy asked her.

"I hate to ask you, Mary, because I know how hard it is for me to deal with, but are you willing to tell me about what happened with your husband?"

Mary heaved a heavy sigh and nodded. "I figured you were going to ask me about Frank the moment you figured out I was speaking from experience. It's been 10 years, and not a single day goes by that I don't find myself thinking about Frank or wondering what he would say or do in a given situation.

"Frank and I grew up together. As kids we did almost everything together, and our parents had been lifelong friends themselves. In many ways, I think falling in love and getting married was inevitable for us, and no one was surprised when our friendship became even more than that.

"At first, we were just friends. I know Frank was already far beyond the friendship stage, but my feelings took a little bit longer to develop into love. I think it had a lot to do with my own teenage ideas about love and marriage, and how the man I would marry was supposed to breeze into town, sweep me off my feet and take me off to his giant mansion for a life of excitement and adventure."

Sandy noticed the wistful smile that had begun to creep across Mary's face, and she knew her friend was lost in her own memories of her dead husband. *Is this the way I look when I speak of Jack?* Sandy wondered. *Do I look as lonely when my own memories fall to my life with my husband?*

Mary's thoughts and memories were interrupted by the telephone, and she immediately snapped back to reality and got up to answer the call. Her voice on the phone didn't betray her emotions, and Sandy could not help but marvel at the inner strength pretending like that must take for Mary. Once the phone call was over, Mary heaved a sigh and then headed into the kitchen for a moment. Sandy was confused at first, but she understood what Mary was doing when she came out with two steaming bowls of stew.

"I did say I was going to eat, didn't I?" Mary said as she placed a bowl in front of Sandy. "This is my secret recipe for caribou stew. People all over the region have come ask me for it, but I have told them there's not enough money in the world for me to give it out."

Sandy picked up her spoon and began to eat. Sandy didn't say much, but Mary could tell the meal was greatly appreciated. For her own reasons, Mary was glad Sandy was distracted for a few short minutes, because then there was no time for any more questions about Frank.

"This is terrific stew, Mary," Sandy said. "Do you think there's any possibility you'd give the recipe to a good friend?"

"I'll tell you what, Sandy. Come back to me and ask just before you leave Holman. Perhaps by then I will have changed my mind. I'm going to go put on another pot of coffee."

Mary got up and hurried back into the kitchen. Sandy knew that Mary was trying to keep the subject away from Frank so she wouldn't have to say more about her own pain. But they both knew the inevitable was only being postponed, and they would no doubt both be in tears by the end.

Mary returned to the table, sat down and heaved yet another heavy sigh. "I know you're waiting for me to continue talking about Frank, but I just need a few more minutes to gather my thoughts."

Sandy reached out to take Mary's hand and smiled. "I more than anyone completely understand, Mary. You take as much time as you need to finish the story."

"We'd been married 10 years. I was at home with the children, and Frank had gone out seal hunting with a few other men from town. They were going to be gone for three days. An unexpected snowstorm blew in from the coast, and they were going to be gone longer than planned because the weather was not good for travelling. I wasn't worried about the delay, because nobody from around here goes out on the land and doesn't bring extra supplies in case of unexpected delays. I knew Frank well enough to know he usually brought along supplies for two or even three more days."

As the memories moved closer and closer to the surface, Sandy saw the look on Mary's face change in an instant. She knew that soon she would have the whole story laid out before her, and Sandy would have to comfort Mary in her time of grief.

"On the third day, I started to get a little bit worried. Frank called me on the trapper radio and said that the weather still hadn't cleared up enough to start back, but they were completely out of supplies and would have to start back regardless of the weather conditions. I told him to be careful, adding that I'd have a pot of caribou stew waiting for him when he got home.

"Four hours after he called me, I fell something inside me break. I couldn't explain it at the time because I didn't understand what it was, but that was the exact moment I lost Frank.

"When the hunting party came home, they were six hours late, and Frank wasn't with them. I was told that while they were on the way back, the storm kicked up once again, and the group got separated. Everyone was able to find each other again, except for Frank. The others spent two hours looking for him, but they decided it was a better idea to come back and get help to look for Frank.

"They looked for Frank for three days. When they found him, he looked like he was sleeping. The look on his face when they brought his body back was one of peace, and I was secretly relieved at knowing that Frank was in a better place now, where he would never be cold again. It broke my heart to know my two boys would grow up without a father, but I knew they would never forget him if it was the last thing I ever did."

No words Sandy could say to Mary would ever be enough to console her, so instead she stayed silent. Even after all this time, Mary's pain was a powerful thing, and Sandy knew that there would be no hope for her to go on as she had before Jack's death. Knowing she was right was little comfort to Sandy, however, because there was a part of her that wanted everyone to be right about her being able to find the strength to move on. If the memories of a lost love were still so powerful for Mary, what hope was there for Sandy to be able to move forward without Jack?

"Does it ever get any easier, Mary? Is there ever a time when you know you'll be strong enough to go on without him?"

"It gets easier, Sandy. I won't lie to you and tell you that you will ever be able to completely forget about the life you shared with Jack, but I will tell you that one day your memories will become a great source of comfort, and what you shared with him will serve to help you better enjoy your life."

"That doesn't give me much hope for my future, Mary. I was hoping for a little something more constructive than the fact that my memories will become a great source of comfort."

"I'm sorry I couldn't give you any better news, but it's important you know the truth. For what it's worth, I can tell you I still celebrate Frank's birthday every year by myself. Sometimes my boys come home to be with me, but most of the time I spend the day alone in my home, flooded with memories of a life I thought would be mine forever and is now nothing more than a painful memory."

Sandy had nothing more to say, and she certainly didn't want to ask any more questions of Mary. Having heard Mary's story of loss, Sandy knew she was not the only person in the world to have suffered a similar fate. For her sake, Sandy had been hoping she could find the key here in Holman. After all her searching, Sandy was beginning to believe her quest had been fruitless.

Chapter 12

So I actually spent two nights alone in the bush in the middle of the Canadian Arctic.

That's right, you did read that last sentence correctly. I, a boy from a big city, spent time in the wilderness by myself. I never thought in a million years that would happen, but of course I never thought I'd be spending my summer in Holman either. I guess I can chalk it up to yet another unbelievable experience.

Perhaps I should explain exactly why I was left alone in the middle of the bush for two days. (I'll need to remember all the details when I want to tell my children the story.) I had gone out with Charlie for a few days away from town to enjoy the nice weather and the fresh air while the weather was holding. Charlie had some free time before the next shipment of housing materials got to town, so he figured this would be the ideal time to get out on the land and maybe do some more fishing and a little bit of hunting if we were really lucky.

We were going to be out for five days, so we had packed up just about everything we thought we would need, including the kitchen sink. We'd also packed up enough food to feed an army for a week, and I couldn't imagine how we were going to get all this stuff out to the camp on the back of two all-terrain vehicles.

Then Charlie pointed out the two sleds we'd pull behind the ATVs, and I knew I had egg on my face. When I made some kind of stupid comment, I almost made Charlie's day from the sound of the laughter alone.

A three-hour trek over rough and rocky terrain wasn't what I'd expected for our expedition, and my butt wasn't all that forgiving when we finally reached Charlie's camp. When I got a better look at where we were going to be spending the next five days, I was surprised.

Calling this place a camp is an understatement. In my opinion, Charlie's camp was more like a rustic cabin. It was obviously built by Charlie, with bits and pieces he'd probably scrounged and stole from the building projects he did around town. Although it looked as if it might fall over at any minute, I knew the cabin would probably never fall down in a hundred years.

The first night at the camp, Charlie regaled me with all sorts of stories of the time he spent here with his father and the rest of his family. The summers were spent on the land, fishing with elders or hunting with his brothers. The men would teach the young boys how to hunt and how to fish, hoping to pass on the skills they had learned to use their entire lives to the next generation and beyond. Charlie also told me about all the stories his father and grandparents had told about life on the Delta, and how things were when the most important part of life was the fishing and hunting and traditional survival methods that had survived thousands of years.

Charlie knew I was scared to death at being out in the middle of nowhere. The last time I'd spent time camping was back when I was in Cubs, and we'd only been 30 minutes from town. Back then there was always someone with a truck who could take us back home if something serious happened. If we needed a couple of stitches, there was someone around who had taken a first aid course and knew how to fix just about anything.

Out in the bush with Charlie, the only person I could rely on was Charlie. If something went wrong, I'd be completely at a loss about what to do. I'd always had other people to rely on in a difficult situation, and I had been accustomed to things being that way. But I knew Charlie was prepared for any eventuality, and I knew that he would know what to do whatever happened.

The next few days were terrific: a lot of fishing, a lot of hunting and a whole lot of laughing. I was having the time of my life, and I was pretty sure that this camping trip would be the highlight of my summer in Holman.

Then one night there was a lot of noise and clatter on the trapper radio, making it impossible for either Charlie or myself to sleep peacefully. When we started listening to what was going on, it became obviously a lot of people seemed to be looking for Charlie. When he finally got up and began trying to contact someone, he found out pretty quickly that everyone had indeed been trying to get hold of him.

Janet had been brought into the nursing post with abdominal pains. They thought she was suffering from appendicitis, but they would have to take her to Inuvik to see a doctor. She knew that Charlie and I were out in the bush, but she needed to see him before she was flown to Inuvik for treatment.

It was the middle of the night, but Charlie wanted to leave immediately. There wasn't enough time to pack everything up and go back to town, so he asked me to stay at the camp until he could come back for the equipment. I wasn't sure I was ready to be alone in the middle of nowhere by myself, but Charlie needed to go, and he needed to know I was going to be fine without him.

I told him to go and not worry about me. He threw on his clothes and went out to check his ATV so he could leave as soon as possible, From the look in his eyes, I could see Charlie's torment: should he stay with me until we were both ready to leave, or should he get back to Holman as quickly as he could? He knew I wasn't near ready to enough to be out there alone, but he needed to see his wife now.

When I told him one more time to go back and see his wife, this time he didn't doubt my confidence. As afraid as I was to be alone, I knew that Janet was the person who needed to be the focus of attention. I'd figure out a way to survive on my own, at least until Charlie could come back to get me.

As I watched Charlie drive off towards town and into the night, I felt the fear begin to creep up to the surface, but I knew I couldn't let it win. If I was going to do anything for Charlie, I had to prove myself. In many ways, the next few days were to be my ultimate test for the rest of my life. That sounds a little overly dramatic, I'm sure. It looks pretty ridiculous to me, and I'm the one who wrote it down. But it wasn't all that far from the truth. If I couldn't manage to take care of myself until Charlie could get back here, I was almost certain I'd never be able to cope in the real world. Here, all I had were my wits and the bare necessities, the minimum anyone would need to survive. I figured that if I could get by now, being alone and left to my own devices back home would be child's play.

The first night was terrible. I couldn't fall asleep to save my life, and my fingers were never more than five inches from Charlie's rifle. But when the sun came up that first time, I began to feel a little stronger and believed I could actually do it. I scrounged through the boxes of food and found enough to make myself a good hearty breakfast, freshly brewed coffee included.

Once breakfast was over, I decided I'd try my luck at fishing. I hadn't become an expert fisherman yet, but Charlie had been telling me I had potential. I had nothing better to do while I was waiting for Charlie to come back, so I picked up my rod and headed for Charlie's fishing spot. Three hours later, I had caught enough fish for lunch and dinner, and probably more than enough to bring a couple of fish home for Janet.

That was when I realized that I had never been one to spend much time alone until this trip to Holman. I always had a lot of people around me, and being on my own was not my idea of a good time. I was never one to be the centre of attention, but being among a large group was always my preference.

Alone at Charlie's camp was probably the best thing that could have ever happened to me. I couldn't hide from my thoughts by using television or radio or anything else to distract myself. I had to deal with the emotions that came to the surface immediately, without delay.

I never had taken the time to face my fears. I never wanted to deal with them, so I managed to push them to the back of my mind. Now, here in the middle of nowhere, I was forced to face the truth—and myself.

Once I had survived the first day, the rest of the time was much easier. When one of Charlie's friends showed up at the camp to help me bring all the stuff back to town, I was glad to see another person. But I also knew that there was still more for me to understand from this experience, and I knew this was only the beginning.

Chapter 13

If Sandy had found herself in a similar-looking house back home, she would have had a great deal of sympathy for such a nice couple barely scraping by from pay cheque to pay cheque.

The small house probably wasn't much bigger than the cottage Sandy's grandparents owned on the lake, and there were many fancy items that would not be found in any house near Sandy's home down south, but it seemed strangely appropriate in this paradise by the ocean.

Did she really just think that? Sandy had only been in Holman one week, yet the reality was this community had already left its mark on her spirit. While her heart was still heavy with grief, her time here had been more therapeutic than Sandy could have hoped for while moping around the house she shared with Jack. She'd made the odd call to her friends to keep them from thinking she'd lost her mind and run off, never to return again. While her friends were still concerned, they were relieved to hear the peace return to Sandy's voice.

"I guess you can't even pretend you'll be coming back to your old life, can you?" said Alison during a late-night telephone call (Sandy had forgotten she was in a different time zone).

"Not at all. When I leave here, I'll be going back to a life without Jack. Before I can find the strength to do that, I have to find out what it was here that gave Jack the strength to be the man I loved and adored from the first time I met him."

"Well, if anyone can find that out, it's you, San."

"Thanks. Listen, I'll call you next week sometime and update you on what I've found out here."

"You know you can call me whenever you need to, don't you?"

Sandy nodded, the tears beginning to fall from her eyes. "I was counting on that, Allie. I was counting on that."

She hung up the phone before she completely broke down. Had she said goodbye? Sandy didn't even know, but she knew that if she'd forgotten, that was yet another habit she had subconsciously picked up in Holman. Every telephone conversation she had heard never ended with a kind goodbye, but with silence.

Time didn't matter all that much around here. Most people didn't even bother wearing a watch, and local events got underway when everyone had shown up and things were in place. For Sandy, not wearing a watch was unsettling at first, but she soon learned to enjoy the relative freedom that not living by the clock allowed her.

Sandy had settled in well the day-to-day events of life in Holman, and she had felt as if she was slowly becoming a part of the family. Every night there were more stories being passed along to her.

She still missed Jack. Although Sandy knew that getting away from her world and the home she shared with Jack was more than necessary for her to continue moving on, she could still feel his presence with her. Perhaps this walk down memory lane was having a more profound effect on her than she'd expected, or perhaps she wasn't ready to move on without Jack yet. Whatever the reason, Sandy took great comfort in the feeling that she wasn't alone.

When she brought up the subject with Charlie and Janet, she was mildly surprised at their positive reactions to what Sandy thought was a clear indication she was losing her mind.

"There's nothing wrong with thinking Jack is still around, Sandy," Janet said. "I think everybody has her own way of dealing with grief. If that's what's helping you get through the day, then I don't see anything wrong with that."

"Why do I get the feeling you don't believe me, Janet?"

Janet heaved a sigh. "I don't know what to believe, frankly, because I have no way of proving or disproving what you're saying."

Sandy turned to look at Charlie. "What do you think? Am I crazy?"

Charlie shook his head and chuckled. "Of all the things I thing you are, crazy isn't one of them. I've heard a lot of people say they've felt comforted by the sense that the person they've lost isn't necessarily gone, but that their essence still remains with us."

"So I guess I shouldn't be booking my stay in a hospital room with nice padded walls just yet."

Charlie replied, "No, Sandy. I think it's safe to say you're about as crazy as the rest of us."

"What do you feel when you think he's around?" asked Janet.

"I'm not sure I can even really explain it. It's not even something I can quantify; it's an overwhelming sense of not being completely alone. It's like knowing there's someone around you, but you can't see them."

"Does it scare you?"

"Not at all. It's a really warm and cosy feeling. I feel as if there's nothing that can hurt me when Jack's around."

"Do you talk to him?"

Sandy smiled hesitantly. "As much as I'm afraid to admit it, I do find myself talking to him. I try to stop myself because it makes me sound crazy, but I can't help wanting to keep him informed about what I'm doing."

Janet returned the smile. "Don't be embarrassed. After finding the man whom you consider your one great love, I can't blame you for trying to keep him close to you. I'd probably do the same thing if I were in your place."

Charlie seemed surprised by his wife's answer, and he arched his eyebrows in response. "Really?"

"Yes, really, Charlie. Don't tell me you're surprised."

"It's just nice to know that you really do love me."

Chapter 14

I just realized I have never been considered an outsider here.

I am not from this place, and neither do I have any experience living in the North, yet the people here have welcomed me with open arms. They have given me a place to stay, they have lent me a warm sweater when I needed one, they have fed me better than I ever imagined and they have never forgotten to invite me along for any community event.

I wonder if I really deserve their hospitality. Compared to most of these people, I am a greenhorn. They have already done more in their lifetimes than I will probably do in 10 lifetimes, if I were to live that long. In their world I am practically nothing, and yet they have never treated me as such.

I never thought I would enjoy my time here. When I first landed here, I was bound and determined to hate this place and everything about it, but the longer I stay here, the less likely it seems that I'll be able to do that. I think I might even be starting to enjoy myself.

Charlie knew that now was the time to tell Sandy the truth. After having talked it over with Janet for quite a while, he knew he couldn't hold off the inevitable for too much longer.

"You know she's going to be angry," Charlie said.

"She'll probably be angry for a while, sweetheart. I think the bigger part of her reaction will be hurt and loss. Sandy came here to find out what she didn't know about her husband, and the whole time she's been spending time with her husband's closest friends here."

"I just hope she'll be able to understand why I didn't tell her the truth from the get go."

Janet stopped her cleaning to sit at the kitchen table with Charlie. She paused before she spoke and reached for her husband's hand. "I can't tell you everything will be fine because I don't know that for sure. What I can tell you is that Sandy will be grateful to know she was able to meet the man who helped Jack become the man with whom she fell in love."

Charlie shook his head and chuckled. "What on earth did I ever do to deserve you?"

"That's easy. You were—and still are—the greatest man I have ever met."

Just as Charlie leaned in to kiss Janet, Sandy entered the kitchen with her empty coffee cup. "I'm sorry. Am I interrupting anything?"

"No, not at all," Janet said. "We were just discussing our plans for the day. I can see your plans include another cup of coffee."

Sandy smiled sheepishly, shrugging her shoulders. "I always feel like I don't get enough caffeine in my day," she joked.

"I know exactly how you feel, Sandy," Charlie said. "There are times when I think there aren't enough hours in a day for a cup of coffee."

Having poured herself another cup, Sandy turned to offer Janet and Charlie their own refills. Janet accepted; Charlie politely refused.

"I was thinking you and I could go visit my camp today, "Charlie said. "I hear the caribou have been hanging around, and I think now is the right time to restock the freezer for the winter."

Sandy nodded. The last time Charlie had invited her to go out to check on something with him, she had discovered that Charlie had something to tell her, and that he wanted to do it in privacy. He had backed off from opening up then, but Sandy had a funny feeling this time would be different. "Sounds like a plan to me. Are you going to come along with us, Janet?"

"I don't think so. I was planning on making caribou stew for dinner, and I like to take my time when I cook stew. You two go on and enjoy yourselves."

"I'm sure we will. When are we leaving, Charlie?"

He didn't answer Sandy right away. "I'll tell you what. You sit here and finish your cup of coffee, and when you're ready to go, I'll be outside."

"You're on."

Charlie left the kitchen, almost visibly relieved to be away from Sandy even if only for a little while. He knew today was going to be emotionally draining for everyone, and he hoped he was strong enough to help Sandy pick up the pieces when she learned of the secret he had been keeping from her.

But Charlie also knew he'd had his reasons. If Sandy was going to be able to overcome her grief, the journey was going to have to happen in its own time. Deep down, Charlie had been aware that the right time to reveal all would one day come, and he would tell Sandy the truth and suffer the consequences—no matter what.

Charlie knew he could wait no longer. His would be the last piece of the puzzle, and hopefully the one piece to help Sandy's heart begin to heal.

The drive out to check the nets was a quiet one. Sandy was lost yet again in the scenery that surrounded her, but Charlie was trying to prepare what he would say. By the time they reached the fish nets, Sandy was certain that checking to see if he'd caught any fish wasn't the only thing on Charlie's mind.

"Okay," Sandy said. "Why don't you tell me the real reason we're out here today, Charlie? I know for a fact you checked your nets just two days ago. That, and Janet told me that you only bring people out with you like this when you have something important to talk about."

"She told you the story about how I proposed to her, didn't she?" he said.

"Yes. But you're still stalling."

Charlie heaved a worried sigh, but the smile on his face betrayed his relief in light of Sandy's words. He was beginning to think that telling Sandy the truth might be a little less painful than he'd expected. "You might want to sit down, because I really don't know how well you're going to react to what I have to say."

Sandy found a rock to sit on, and she pulled her knees to her chest. "You're scaring me, Charlie. Why do I get the feeling I won't like what you have to say?"

Charlie began pacing nervously as he tried to decide where to start. "First of all, I want you to know that I have enjoyed the time we have spent together here in Holman. Being able to show you the way of life here, and you responding in such a wonderful and open manner, has been something to see. Although we have only known each other a short time, I hope you know you have become like family to me."

"I feel exactly the same way, Charlie."

"I also want you to know that I would never hurt you on purpose, and that anything I have kept from you until now was for your own good, because I thought it was best."

Sandy reached for Charlie's hand to stop him from pacing any further. "Whatever it is you have to tell me, I think you had better just spit it out."

Charlie nodded then took a deep breath. "I knew Jack when he was here in Holman, and I was the one who took him under my wing."

Sandy smiled brightly, secretly relieved that the only thing Charlie was confessing was something she had already known. She had initially thought about playing up her emotions, but the panicked look on Charlie's face made her think otherwise. "That's it? That's your big confession?"

Charlie nodded nervously. "I've been trying to tell you for days. I could never find the guts to tell you I'd been lying to you. I know you came here for answers, and my keeping secrets from you makes that impossible."

Sandy reached over and placed a calming hand on Charlie's arm. "Don't. I'm not angry with you. It's all right. I understand."

Immediately a relieved smile crossed Charlie's face. She didn't hate him—this time. "You don't know how happy I am to hear you say that, Sandy. I thought I was going to ruin your entire trip when you found out I was lying to you about knowing Jack."

"Something tells me that you were trying to allow me the time to see this place before giving all the facts. And it's fine."

Charlie heaved a sigh. He had only just begun to tell Sandy the things she needed to know, but even a small part of the story could help Sandy heal her broken heart. There were still things he knew she needed to learn, and Charlie hoped she would take them in stride as she had this first admission.

He straightened his shoulders and cleared his throat. "Well, now that we've taken care of that, we have one more thing to do before heading out to the camp."

Sandy smiled and gave Charlie a hug. She wanted to make sure that he knew things were still fine between them. At the same time, she was mentally kicking herself for thinking that Charlie would ever keep anything of significance from her; she knew him better than that.

Sandy followed Charlie back to his truck. She climbed into the passenger seat and then playfully gave Charlie a punch in the shoulder. He shook his head and put the key into the ignition.

"So, where are we going?" she asked.

"Huh?"

"Five minutes ago you told me you had one more thing to do before we could head out to your camp. I just asked you where we were going."

"Oh. We I have to go pick up my nephew. He's been staying with my sister since you got to Holman, simply because we didn't want you to feel too overwhelmed while you were staying with us."

"Your nephew? How old is he?"

"Tommy just turned five last month. He's lived with Janet and me since his mother died. His school day is just about to finish, and I told my sister I'd pick him up from school."

"You know, Charlie, you didn't have to send him away just because I was coming to stay with you. I would not have minded your nephew being around."

"He can be a bit of a handful, even on his best days. Besides, he loves visiting my sister because she spoils him all the time. I was going to bring him along on our trip, if you don't mind."

Sandy shook her head. "Not at all. It will be nice to have the chance to see your camp through the eyes of someone who isn't too jaded yet."

Charlie smiled brightly. "Tommy's the best little helper I could have ever asked for. He's not all that strong yet, but he never gives up without a fight. He's going to make one heck of a fisherman when he gets older."

"You must be happy you have someone to pass on your knowledge to. That must be such a great feeling."

"It really is. Sometimes when I look at him, I miss his mother a lot and wish she could be here to see him grow, but then I know that if she was here, I wouldn't be spending so much time with him."

Sandy didn't respond immediately, because she was lost in her own thoughts about Charlie's last statement. *Everything does happen for a reason,* she thought to herself. If she'd never lost Jack, she never would have met Charlie and all the good people here. If she was supposed to lose Jack, exactly what was she supposed to gain from that? "You must feel very lucky, Charlie. I think I envy you."

"You won't envy me when I'm an old man trying to keep a handle on a growing boy," Charlie replied. Sandy wasn't surprised to hear only warmth in his voice.

The truck pulled up to the school, and Charlie quickly jumped out. Sandy also decided to get out, but she wasn't as quick to react. She hesitantly moved over to where Charlie was standing to wait for Tommy.

The school bell rang, and children began pouring out of the front doors of the school. Sandy watched as Charlie scanned the faces of the boys and girls heading home, looking for Tommy.

"Tommy! Tommy!"

A beautiful little boy with dark hair looked up at the sound of Charlie's voice. He began to run towards his uncle, smiling. Charlie swept the young boy up into his arms. "Ungung! Auntie never told me you were coming to get me. Does this mean I can go back home with you?"

"Yep! That's why I came to pick you up today, because I couldn't wait to bring you back. Do you want to come out to the camp with me and my friend Sandy?"

"Do you mean it? I've wanted to go back to the camp forever! Can we go now?"

Charlie chuckled. "You betcha. As soon as I introduce you to my friend."

He stretched out his hand to Tommy. Sandy noticed the slightest hesitation on Charlie's part, which she found to be odd. Slowly, Charlie and Tommy made their way to where Sandy was standing.

Charlie cleared his throat, just as he had before admitting to Sandy that he had known Jack during his time here. "Sandy, I would like to introduce you Tommy."

Sandy took a closer look at Tommy and gasped.

She was looking straight into the eyes of her dead husband.

Chapter 15

How is it possible that I have never been farther from everything I knew in my life and yet still feel like I am perfectly at home here? Here, in this place where I am in the minority. Where hardship exists on a completely different level than I ever realized. Where total darkness takes on a completely different meaning for these people. And where people open their hearts and share what little they have with each other including a stranger like me.

I finally understand what my parents wanted me to understand by spending my summer here. It is quite possible to live a full and satisfying life without having to have all the latest toys and gadgets. In this world, no one cares if you have the fanciest cars or the nicest house. What's more important is your abilities and talents when it comes to hunting. If you can tell them exactly where they should go to catch a caribou or where the fish are running, that is more valuable to them than having the latest big thing. If you can help them survive and prepare for the harsh months of winter, you will have greater standing in this community than if you were making a seven-figure salary.

Money doesn't matter here. They have enough to live on, and if they run short, there are ways to get around the problem. In a world where so much is based on getting ahead and making a quick buck, the people of Holman are more interested in the value of the people surrounding them—and they are truly more blessed than I ever thought possible.

And now that I've seen it for myself, I'm beginning to think it might be possible in my own life at some point in the future.

If Sandy had been punched hard in the stomach, the look on her face would have been similar to the expression she now wore. Almost immediately after Charlie's confession, Sandy backed away, needing to get away from Charlie and take some time to let what she had just heard sink in. This was certainly not what Sandy had been expecting to hear. If she had stayed even a minute longer with Charlie, there would have been harsh words exchanged on both sides, and a fledgling friendship would have been destroyed on the spot. As angry as she was for having been deceived been by one whom she had come to trust, Sandy also sensed there was more to the story. Now was not the time to get the answers; now was the time for distance.

"I think you had better take me back, Charlie. There is no way in hell I'm going to stay out here in the middle of nowhere with you—certainly not tonight."

Charlie nodded, knowing that she was right. As Sandy made her way over to the truck to sit in the passenger side, Charlie picked up Tommy and helped him into the cab. He got into the driver's seat, turned his truck around and headed back to town.

The silence on the drive back was deafening, and every minute the silence went on was one more minute for Charlie to be worried. He knew Sandy was mad, and he knew she had every right to be, but he hoped that she might understand why he didn't tell her the truth from the start. But if she wasn't even going to talk to him, there was little chance of the two of them being able to work things out.

The minute Charlie pulled up in front of the house, Sandy got out of the truck and stormed off, obviously still needing time alone to think about what she had just discovered. Charlie didn't bother to follow Sandy, because he knew she would need time before she was ready to react. He fell into Janet's warm and welcoming embrace.

"Are you okay?" Janet asked.

"She hates me," Charlie said as he shook his head. "She's never going to talk to me again."

"You knew this wasn't going to be a smooth ride, honey. Sandy needs time to deal with what you just told her. Once she has come to terms with it, she will understand why you did what you did."

"Suppose she never forgives me. What if she comes to hate everything she has experienced on this trip simply because I was trying to protect her?"

Janet smiled slightly. She had expected a reaction like this from Charlie, and she knew better than anyone how his guilt would work against him once Sandy learned the truth. Janet also knew she was the only person who could help Charlie see that all was not yet lost.

"Charlie, you have spent every day with Sandy for three weeks. Do you honestly believe she is the kind of person who won't forgive you?"

Charlie smiled then kissed Janet tenderly on the cheek. "What would I do without you?"

"That's not even worth thinking about. You and I both know that isn't going to happen. Now, which way did Sandy run off after you told her the truth?"

"Towards the church. She knows it's open, and I would think it's empty at this time of day."

Janet nodded. "You stay here. There's fresh coffee and plenty of leftovers in the fridge. I'll go over and talk to her."

Charlie nodded and then headed into the house.

Janet took a deep breath, pulling her hair back into place. As she headed for the church, Janet tried to plan out what she was going to say to Sandy. If Sandy was mad at Charlie because he did not tell her the truth, then Janet was also at fault.

When Janet had first met Jack, Janet had thought him to be nothing special—just another kid from down south who was looking for his own northern experience. She figured Jack would spend his three or four months in Holman and then go home and tell everyone about living in the Arctic.

For his part, Jack didn't make anything all that easy in the early days of his time here. Even though Charlie and Janet were opening their home and their lives to him, Jack was angry, brooding and miserable for days. He didn't want to be here, and he was bound and determined to make everyone pay for his misery.

There wasn't much for Charlie and Janet to do but to go about their business, hoping Jack would change his mind. Janet knew that sooner or later, Jack was going to come around—or he was going to call his father and be on a plane out of here.

It was three days later that Jack finally gave in.

Janet was baking in the kitchen, busily trying to do three tasks at the same time, when she saw a shadow in the kitchen doorway out of the corner of her eye. She wasn't sure Jack knew she could see him, but Janet wasn't going to scare him off.

Finally, Jack cleared his throat. "I owe you an apology," he said.

That was not what Janet had expected as the first words out his mouth. She nearly dropped the egg in her hand. "An apology? Whatever for, Jack?"

"For being a jerk from the moment I walked through your front door. For hiding in my room and moping. For being an idiot. You and Charlie deserve better from me."

"I know this isn't necessarily your idea of an ideal summer vacation spot, but I promise you that if you give it a try, you won't be sorry."

"I really am sorry, Janet. I am usually not as rude as I have been since my arrival here, but I will admit I had some plans for this summer before my father told me he was sending me about as far north as I could possibly go. I know he and Charlie had met a while back, and my dad thought I needed to grow up, but this wasn't my plan. But since I am here, I think I should make an effort to experience everything I can. I mean, who knows when I'll ever get back up here again?"

Janet smiled. "That's the spirit. I know you won't regret it, Jack."

From that day on, Janet was pleasantly surprised to discover there was much more to Jack than she had thought. He was beginning to see the man he could be, and having the chance to be exposed to a simpler way of life would serve him well in the future. By the time Jack left to return to his life in the south, Janet knew she had made a friend for life and that she had been fortunate enough to see Jack grow into a great man.

And what Janet knew from Sandy, Jack had in fact become a great man. His life may not have been long enough, but Jack had left a considerable mark on this world through the people who were an important part of his life.

By the time Janet reached the church, she had a pretty good idea of what she was going to say to Sandy. She quietly entered the church and sat in the pew directly behind Sandy.

"Are you okay?" Janet asked.

"I'll survive."

"You know, Sandy, I think your husband was one of the finest men I have ever known."

"Thank you," Sandy said without thinking. Once Janet's words began to sink in, Sandy turned around, glaring. "You knew Jack too, didn't you?"

Janet nodded. "Jack was here the summer Charlie and I got married. As a matter of fact, Jack was here for the wedding.

"We weren't going to let you leave without telling you, if that's what you're thinking," Janet said. "We just wanted to wait for a good time."

Sandy shook her head.

"And now is a good time? What the hell makes now a good time to tell me?"

Janet moved up to sit beside Sandy and took her hand. As the tears fell once again from Sandy's eyes, Janet tenderly wiped them away. "We thought it was more important for you to see Holman for yourself before you knew the real story. Charlie thought that seeing this place through Jack's eyes would have been unnecessarily painful for you, and we both know he was right. You simply weren't ready for that when you first got here, because you were nowhere near strong enough. He and I wanted you to gain a little bit of strength before we told you the truth about Jack."

Sandy didn't know how to respond to Janet's revelation. How could Charlie and Janet have lied to her? They knew how much Sandy wanted— no, needed—to know about Jack's time here. In fact, she had made no secret of her reasons for taking this trip to Holman, and she'd secretly hoped everyone would simply tell her the answers from the first time she met them. Wasn't it supposed to be that easy?. "That's no excuse for lying to me!"

"You see it as lying, Sandy. But we were always going to tell you once we thought you were ready to hear it. I'm not trying to make excuses; I'm being completely honest with you."

Even though she wanted to argue, Sandy heard the sincerity in Janet's voice. But that wasn't about to change the situation. Sandy had been lied to. By Charlie. By Janet. By Jack. What else had been a lie about her time here?

"Sandy, please. Please let us try and explain. Let Charlie explain."

"Janet, he's had more than enough time to explain it to me. Why should I give him any more time?"

Janet had figured Sandy would be angry, but she had not expected Sandy to close herself off so quickly. They needed to sit down and talk this out, because everybody needed to explain themselves. Janet carefully reached out to place a hand on Sandy's shoulder, but Sandy shrugged it away.

"You're angry. I get that, Sandy. And Charlie gets that. We just want to be given the chance to explain, to tell you our side of the story."

"I can't do it right now, Janet. I can't listen to you and Charlie talk about Jack right now."

Janet nodded in understanding. "Fair enough. But you have to promise you will let us explain everything before you leave town. You owe it to Jack to find out everything before you leave Holman."

"That's not playing fair, Janet."

Janet allowed a smile to cross her face. There was still hope that Sandy would listen to them. "Tell you what. Why don't you and I go over to the hotel? I'll get Mary to give you a room, and you can take some time to digest everything you have just found out. When you're ready, Charlie and I will be more than willing to answer all of your questions."

"Will there be any rooms available tonight? Mary isn't expecting me."

Janet raised a hand to caress Sandy's face and smiled brightly. "I told Charlie to call Mary and get everything organized before I came over here to find you."

Sandy should have known Charlie wouldn't leave to her own devices, even if she wasn't talking to him right now. She nodded and then walked down the centre aisle of the church.

Janet heaved a heavy sigh of relief, following closely behind Sandy.

Chapter 16

Charlie and Jane are like the ideal couple, if you ask me. Not that I know much about being a happy couple, mind you. But when I look at the two of them, I know they are perfect for each other.

Charlie is very much a man of his environment: he's a good hunter, is an even better fisherman and is considered by many the best tracker in many years. He can fix just about anything that is broken, whether or not he's ever seen it before. Quite honestly, if I am even half the man he is, I'll be a very happy camper.

As for Jane, her only goal in life is to take care of her husband. She can cook an eight-course meal, sew the most exquisite wedding gown in no time flat and can make you feel like the most important person on the planet. But above all, she has an inner beauty that is simply stunning.

I have a feeling I will never find a woman like Jane anywhere else in the world, even if I spent a lifetime searching for her. The girls I have met in my life may turn out to be terrific women, but none of them will ever hold a candle to Jane or any of the other women in this place. Sure, the girls back home want someone to adore them, but they also are all determined to remain as independent as possible within the relationship. Back home, the girls have been all taught to strive to achieve for themselves and be self-sufficient if the need ever arises.

The women like Jane do learn what they need to survive, but their biggest source of joy and pleasure comes from marriage and children. If their family is happy and healthy, there is nothing more they need to do, and there is nothing left to prove. Family is the most important thing to anyone in Holman, and there is nothing that ranks any higher. If there is a family emergency, there is absolutely no question that everything else can wait until whatever has happened is taken care of, and there is no further discussion on the matter. Not to say that family isn't important everywhere, but in a lot of places in today's society, the family must learn to deal with whatever happens while people are at work or are busy doing other things; family counts as number one, but only when it's convenient in a lot of cases. Here, it's family first, and the rest can just damn well wait.

The second he stepped through the doors of the hotel, Charlie knew he had his work cut out for him. Three days had passed since Sandy had learned what Charlie and Janet had been keeping from her, and those days had passed without even the slightest word from Sandy. The only thing Charlie could remember was the look of total heartbreak and betrayal that had crossed Sandy's face as she put the pieces together.

As he stepped towards the dining room, Charlie heard a booming voice from the kitchen. "What in the hell did you do to that poor woman, Charlie?" The kitchen doors swung wide open, and Mary approached him. She could see by the look on his face that Sandy knew the truth about everything. "She knows, doesn't she? Sandy found out about Tommy."

All Charlie could do was nod. He moved over to one of the tables and sat down heavily.

Mary heaved a sigh and sat down beside her cousin. "Tell me what happened."

"It was my fault. I thought it was time for me to come clean, to tell her the truth before it was too late. But I couldn't find the right words to explain to her about Jack and Tommy ... and Alice."

Mary nodded, not wanting to interrupt Charlie's flow. She knew all too well how hard it was for him to even say his daughter's name, so if she was going to brought up here, she was going to let Charlie guide the conversation.

"I had tried and tried to figure out a way to tell Sandy easily about what had happened between Jack and Alice, but I couldn't find the words. Janet told me that Alice would want Sandy to know the truth, and I knew that the longer I waited, the less time Sandy would have to let it sink in and get the answers she needed to move on. When Jessie couldn't pick up

Tommy from school on Monday because she had a dentist appointment, I thought that would be the perfect time. Sandy and I had been all over town doing little errands and odd jobs, so stopping to pick up someone at the school didn't seem too out of place."

"But you were picking up Tommy. Did Sandy know who you were picking up?"

Charlie shook his head. "No. I was going to drop him off at home with Janet, and then I was going to tell Sandy everything. But she figured it all out before I had the chance to explain."

"How?" Mary asked, reaching for Charlie's hand to offer support.

"She looked at Tommy's eyes."

Mary nodded. She had always said the very same thing about that beautiful little boy: he had his father's beautiful, warm, kind brown eyes. It would have been hard for Sandy not to recognize them.

"I screwed it all up, Mary. Everything is ruined. Jack and Alice would both be disappointed in me."

"Stop right there. You took care of that boy when no one else could. You loved him as if he was your own son. Neither Jack nor Alice would have ever been angry with you. Charlie, you were raising that boy to be a great man. No one could have asked for more."

Charlie stood up and began to pace. "And Sandy? How do you think she feels about me now? She trusted me to help her find the answers she needed, and I was hiding the biggest truth of them all! I betrayed her in the worst possible way."

"Sandy will understand. She simply needs time to let it all sink in, Charlie. Can you imagine what that must have been like for her? To have come all this way to find out more about the man she married, only to come face to face with the son she never knew he'd had? A son he'd had with someone else."

"I'm not so sure, Mary. You didn't see the look in her eyes when she walked away from me. I haven't seen or heard from her in three days, and quite frankly I wouldn't be surprised if I never heard from her again."

"So you haven't heard from her since she checked back in here?"

Charlie shook his head. "No. As soon as she ran off, Janet went after her and eventually found her sitting in the church. They talked for a little bit, and Janet tried to explain everything, even the truth she had been hiding from Sandy. But there was no way Sandy was going to come back to the house. Janet said Sandy left the church first and headed here. I was so sure she was going to try to get herself on the first available flight and never return—or forgive any of us."

The night that Sandy had checked back into the hotel, Mary had tried her best to find out what had happened between her and Charlie. Mary had figured out for herself what had happened, but she had hoped that if she were able to get Sandy to open up to her, Mary could fix things between Charlie and Sandy pretty quickly.

That wasn't going to be the case. Sandy had locked herself in her room ever since she'd returned to the hotel. The only reason Sandy had left the room was to use the bathroom, and it was clear she did not want to talk to anyone. The "Do Not Disturb" card had been hanging on the door, and the only sound anyone heard coming from the room was the sound of Sandy crying. Even though she hadn't asked for anything, Mary was sure to leave food outside the door, just in case Sandy got hungry. No one had seen her take the trays inside the room, but they had seen the empty plates stacked neatly on the tray outside in the hallway for removal.

This was what Mary had warned Charlie about. She had told him that if Sandy found out the truth in the wrong way, the reaction would be extreme. But he had thought Sandy would be level-headed enough to want to discuss things rationally.

That only proved how little Charlie understood the depth of Sandy's pain. Having gone through it herself when Frank had died, Mary knew that the pain would never truly go away, and there would never be a time that Sandy would be able to discuss Jack in a calm, rational manner. It simply wasn't possible in a situation like this one. Sandy would find the strength to move on, but this was one wound that would never fully heal.

"I told you, Charlie. I told you to be honest with her. I told you to this would go wrong if you didn't handle it properly."

Charlie sat back down at the table, somewhat calmer about the situation. "Yes, you did tell me. You told me exactly how this would go down. In fact, I think you even told me you were going to keep her room free just in case she needed it. How did you know?"

"Do you honestly have to ask me that, Charlie? You of all people should understand how it is I knew exactly how she was going to react to this story."

He nodded slowly. "Frank. But that was, what, 15 years ago?"

"It will be 17 years on Friday, Charlie. And it could have been 117 years since I lost Frank, and I would still understand Sandy's reaction. That is what I was trying to get across to you on her very first night here. It doesn't matter how much time has passed—it still hurts."

"How do I fix this, Mary? How do I make sure she understands?"

Mary reached out here hand to grab Charlie's and squeezed it gently.

"Leave it to me, big brother. I will make sure you get your chance to explain."

Chapter 17

So this is it.

I've survived an entire summer living in the middle of nowhere. I have never been more isolated than I was for the last two months, and I have never been farther from home in my entire life.

Yet somehow, I can't imagine another adventure ever measuring up to what I have experienced in Holman.

As the plane taxied down the runway to takeoff, I suddenly realized I hadn't taken one photograph the entire time I was in Holman. It's not that I didn't bring a camera with me; to be quite honest, I have a very nice camera. I never took a single photograph because I think on some level I knew the image would never truly capture the moment. Even the most fantastic photograph would pale in comparison to what I picture in my mind. I could have taken a thousand photos, and none would have truly done my summer in Holman justice.

And that's probably why I am going home with a fresh roll of film in my camera. There is no photograph I could have taken that would have made people understand what this summer has meant to me. I'm sure none of my friends will believe me when I tell them my stories. I know what my initial reactions were like, so it's not all that hard to visualize how those who have known me best will react. They will be in awe and disbelief, and perhaps question my sanity when I tell them of how I enjoyed living in Holman, and they will be astounded by my love and respect for a part of the world I still know very little about.

But that is one thing I learned this summer. Once a place like Holman gets under your skin, you are powerless to keep it from infusing your entire being. There will never be a day that goes by where I will not think of these past few months. I will no doubt share stories of my days in Holman and the friends I have made for years to come. In the future, I will use what limited knowledge I now have of the Canadian North to better educate my friends and those people I meet on a regular basis, and maybe I'll put some of these rumours and myths about life in the North to rest.

When I finally meet the woman I am destined to spend the rest of my life with, I will fascinate her with tales of my Arctic adventure. She will be the one person I will share every detail and every experience, and she will be the one who will come to truly understand what this summer has meant to me and to the man I have become. She is the person I will bring back to Holman so that she can see this place for herself and live through the same experience I did this past summer.

And I know she's going to love Charlie.

As she lay in her bed, Sandy knew she really needed to get up and face the day. Three days of hiding was enough.

Charlie's betrayal—everyone's betrayal—had hit her hard because she had never seen it coming. Most times when she was going to be broadsided by something, Sandy had always had a feeling that something wasn't quite right.

This time, she'd never seen any of the signs.

Even Jack had betrayed her, from beyond the grave. The one person Sandy had always thought had been completely honest with her had been keeping the biggest secret of all—and he took it with him to the grave.

A son. A beautiful little boy with Jack's eyes.

The one thing she would never share with Jack, and the one thing she had desperately wanted. They had always talked about having kids someday, but Jack kept saying he wasn't ready, that he needed more time to put a few things in place before he would be ready to take this step. Sandy had tried to be understanding, but she had started to think that maybe Jack wasn't interested in having children at all.

But obviously that could not have been further from the truth, because there was already a child of his in the world living his life thousands of kilometres away from Jack, living life like nothing he would have experienced in the big city.

Did Jack even know? If he had known, for how long? How long was he planning to keep it a secret from Sandy? Was Jack ever going to tell her the truth?

Right now, Sandy had nothing but questions. If she wanted to find out the real story, there was only one option: get up and face those who had been lying to her from the first moment she'd come here.

This place had always felt so open and honest. Now, Sandy realized that it was a place full of secrets, mysteries and stories and tales—and lies. There had been not one person who had been telling her the entire story since she got here. They had been lying about knowing Jack, they had been lying about what happened to Jack while he was here and they had been lying when they had claimed they were telling Sandy the whole story.

She wasn't sure why she was so angry with people whom, if Sandy were being completely honest with herself, didn't really know all that well. Sure, everyone in town had been pretty friendly and more than welcoming (except for Peter), but they had mentioned to Sandy they were pretty familiar with the idea of people coming here to get something for themselves and then leaving. Perhaps Sandy had given off some sort vibe, and everyone had realized they should keep Tommy' existence from her. She'd be gone soon enough, back to her little life in the south and none the wiser that Jack's son was running around the dusty streets, learning to fish and hunt, making the friends who would be with him for a lifetime and making a life for himself with his grandparents.

But Sandy couldn't accept that. Jack's friend owed her an explanation, and she was not about to leave without it.

She got out of bed and stretched. Getting out of bed was now her biggest accomplishment in a number of days. She stretched and then headed to her suitcase. She pulled out the first thing she found that was clean. Dressing quickly, Sandy brushed her teeth and ran a brush through her hair. She took a deep breath and then opened her hotel room door.

As usual, the corridor was eerily quiet. Sandy quietly made her way towards the dining room but stopped before stepping inside. The first person she was going to face was Mary. The one face Sandy had always loved seeing first thing in the morning, because there was always a big smile gracing it. The one person who had made Sandy feel comfortable. The one person who Sandy felt understood her heartache.

The first step was always the hardest. Sandy took a deep breath and stepped into the dining room. Mary wasn't anywhere to be seen, so Sandy headed towards what had become her usual table and sat down.

The relative peace and quiet of the dining room was welcome; Sandy wished she could say the same for her inner voice. She was angry and knew that she had good reason to be angry with just about everyone she had met since the day she had arrived, but that did not stop her from feeling bad about the way she had lashed out at Charlie.

"It's good to see you coming out of your room again, Sandy."

Startled by the sudden voice, Sandy turned around to find Mary in the doorway of the kitchen. Mary's tentative smile made Sandy fell somewhat guilty, knowing that she was the reason for the hesitation from someone whom Sandy regarded as a friend. Sandy stood up and approached Mary, who looked as if she expected the worst.

"Mary, I am so sorry. In my grief and in my anger, I lashed out at all of you and was more than ready to leave here and never look back. I never should have behaved the way I did, because that benefits no one."

Mary heaved a sigh of relief and smiled brightly. Sandy relaxed a bit as well in that moment, and she instinctively moved to warmly embrace Mary.

"What happened, Sandy? What's changed your mind about all this?"

Sandy took Mary's hand and guided her to one of the tables in the restaurant. As Mary sat down, Sandy walked over to the corner and picked up two mugs and the fresh pot of coffee sitting on the burner.

Sandy poured the coffee, and Mary wiped a tear from her cheek.

"I really am sorry, Mary. I usually don't behave the way that I did. I was just so …"

"Angry?"

Sandy shook her head. "No. Jealous."

Mary was stunned. Of all the answers she had expected from Sandy, that wasn't one of them. The obvious answer was anger, because Sandy had been lied to by those people she had met here, and they had all known the reason for Sandy's visit: to find the answers she needed in order to move forward with her life. When Sandy realized she wasn't getting the whole story, there was no doubt anger, and Mary didn't begrudge her that.

"Jealous? Sandy, whatever for?"

"Because Jack had a child without me. Because you had all been lucky enough to know Jack's son before me. Because I would never get to have that."

"Sandy, there is no saying you won't have a child of your own one day. I know you had always imagined Jack as your child's father, but perhaps that is not what the universe has planned for you. We never should have kept that from you, that Jack had a son, but we didn't know how to broach the subject with you."

"I deserved the truth! Did any of you think about that?"

"Sandy, "Mary said, "how on earth we were supposed to give you the truth when it was clear that you would not have dealt with all that just yet? I told Charlie he needed to come clean, but I couldn't push him. The truth still hurts him, and he deals with it every day. Having to talk about it with someone he really doesn't know all that well is asking a lot of him. You have to know that much. Or maybe you are just here for yourself."

Sandy felt even worse for having been so angry with everyone, knowing that they were simply trying to figure out how to tell her the truth without adding to her pain and heartache. If she hadn't been so focused on her own pain, she'd have been able to see the bigger picture. She had been grieving for a few months now, but the people here had only been grieving since Sandy's arrival.

"I get that, Mary. I've been so selfish. You, Charlie and everyone else are grieving for Jack as well, and I should know better than to take it out on you. I never meant to hurt any of you."

"Of course you didn't! You had just found out one of the biggest secrets your husband had—one that he took with him to his grave. That must have been so terrible for you."

Sandy nodded her head. That Mary understood a little bit about the headspace she was in made Sandy feel better, but there was still work to be done. If Sandy was going to get the answers she wanted, she needed to make things right, and Mary was probably the easiest place to start. If Mary was back on her side, the rest would be a whole lot easier for Sandy.

"It doesn't make my behaviour any less ridiculous, Mary. I shouldn't have taken my hurt and anger out on you and Charlie and Jane."

Mary didn't respond but nodded her head slowly. Sandy knew she had a lot of bridges to mend, and fixing what she had broken would take time. She wasn't quite sure she would have enough time to fix all that she had broken. But she knew Jack would never forgive her if she didn't try to fix things. If she were being completely honest with herself, there were still a few answers she was going to need before she left town.

The Jack she knew, that was. This new Jack that Sandy was meeting, the one who had kept the biggest secret of his life from her, was a stranger. Sandy took another sip of her coffee, which gave her a bit of time to think about her next response.

"I just need to understand. How could this secret be true, Mary? How could Jack, my husband, have kept this from me? This is not the man I knew, the man I married. He'd never keep this secret from me. Why wouldn't he have told me? It makes no sense!"

Sandy got up from the table and began to pace. She was angry, but she'd spent enough time lashing out at people, and she needed to release the energy somehow. She didn't know what else to do.

She realized that the one person who could perhaps explain—maybe the only one she could trust to tell her the truth—was Charlie. He had known Jack the best, and he could tell Sandy the real story.

But would Charlie even talk to her anymore? After the way she'd walked away without giving him a chance, would he be willing to give *her* a chance to apologize? The only way Sandy would know would be to find Charlie and get him to talk to her.

"How angry is Charlie?" Sandy asked Mary.

"He was never angry with you, only hurt. All he wanted was the opportunity to explain his reasons for not being completely honest with you, because that was what was most important to him. He was never going to let you leave without an explanation. Charlie was always going to tell you the truth before you left; he was waiting for what he thought was the right moment. What you need to realize is that while you lost a husband when Jack died, Charlie lost the closest thing he ever had to a brother. Only he didn't know it until you came to town. I think you can help each other out now."

Sandy didn't respond. Her thoughts returned to Jack, as they always did. She wished Jack could have told her about Tommy before he'd died, because then she would have a better idea of how she should react in this situation. He had long been her sounding board, and she could use one of those right now.

Jack had always been honest with her in all aspects—except when it came to his time here. She was beginning to see why he had not told her about all this, because she had a feeling that he had been waiting for the perfect time.

"I wish Jack was here to tell me what I'm supposed to do," Sandy said.

Mary reached her hand across the table to touch Sandy. "He's still with you, Sandy. Everything that Jack ever did for you or taught you or told you is still with you. Just because he's gone, that doesn't mean he can't be a part of your life."

Sandy sat quietly, letting Mary's words sink in. She thought it a bit odd she had never looked at her current situation that way, but she chalked it up to grief. She had spent so much time feeling sorry for herself that she wasn't able to see the bigger picture: she wasn't alone. Even if Jack wasn't here, he was still helping her make the choices she needed to make. He was still the one voice rolling around in her head to which she listened for guidance. She still wondered, *What would Jack do?* when it came down to decision time. He was still with her every step of the journey. She wasn't alone.

Chapter 18

Once the full force of that realization became clear to Sandy, the emotion hit her like a runaway train. The feelings were just as powerful as they had been on the day she had received the telephone call from Officer Jameson telling her about the accident. They were just as powerful as they had been when she stood by Jack's graveside and watched as his coffin was lowered into the ground.

Now, there was something else mixed in with the emotions. Amongst the heartbreak, pain, agony, regret and fury was a sense of peace, almost serenity. Sandy still felt Jack's loss just as strongly, yet there was a new feeling of hope. She had hope she might be able to find a way to go on without the one person she once thought she would never be able to live without.

Mary said, "What's going on in that head of yours, Sandy? The look in your eyes has completely changed."

Sandy was startled. She had forgotten that she was not alone in the restaurant.

"You just got it, didn't you, Sandy? You just realized that Jack may have died, but he's never going to leave you."

"Yeah. I can't understand it or explain it, but your words finally sunk in. I know you're not the first person who has said them to me, but you are the only one that managed to get through. Why?"

"I don't know," Mary said, shaking her head. "I can't explain it either. Maybe because your heart recognized that I truly understood what you were going through. Perhaps because you were finally ready to accept the truth. For whatever reason, I am glad that it has finally happened, because now the healing can start. Now you can truly begin to move forward."

"I wish I was as certain as you are, Mary. I'm not sure I am there just yet."

Mary nearly dropped her coffee mug, staring at Sandy in amazement. "Don't be ridiculous. Remember where you are sitting at this very moment."

Sandy was puzzled for about 30 seconds. Then she realized Mary was absolutely right. She had taken the biggest risk of her life and travelled to a completely different part of the country alone, in order to try to better understand Jack and his life before they knew one another. She had found the strength within herself to keep putting one foot in front of the other and move forward.

Without Jack. The one person she thought she could not survive without. She already had begun to move forward, alone. And yet she was not completely alone.

Now finally understanding just about everything, Sandy knew there was so much more she needed to know, and there was only one person that could help her find the answers which she still needed.

"Do you think Charlie will forgive me, Mary? I was so horrible to him."

"My brother is the most level-headed person on the planet. Why do you think he waited so long to tell you the truth about knowing Jack? Because he knew that you would be furious, but more important, you would be really hurt by his silence. Charlie will understand, Sandy. He loved Jack too."

Sandy nodded. She hoped that Mary was right and that her new friend would forgive her. Sandy looked at the time and knew that Mary got up ridiculously early every morning. She stood up from her chair and stretched. "I think we had better call it a night. You need to get to bed."

Mary smiled at Sandy. "You're right. I hadn't noticed the time; I was having too much fun sitting around chatting with you. Tomorrow if you go looking for Charlie, try the town garage. I heard him mention at lunch that he needed to do some work on his truck's brakes."

Sandy hugged Mary tightly. "You're too good to me—all of you. I'm not sure I deserve any of you."

Sandy turned around quickly and headed for her room, knowing tomorrow was going to be an emotionally charged day for her and Charlie.

Mary was too stunned by her new friend's words to respond before Sandy disappeared. She wiped away a tear from her left cheek before picking up the mugs and returning them to the kitchen. Mary picked up her bags, headed for the door and turned out the lights. She looked up to the ceiling and whispered into the darkness.

"She's going to be just fine, Jack. You picked a strong woman. She's not going to give up now."

Before Mary could receive any kind of mysterious sign, she headed out.

Chapter 19

This place is fantastic. I've never been further from civilization, and yet I've never been more at home. I've come to realize that I don't need much to keep myself happy, but there are some things that I know I will never need. I don't need a lot of money. I will need enough for the bare necessities, but I don't necessarily need a lot of stuff to clutter up my life. If I keep my worldly possessions to a minimum, then if I have to pack up and move again, I'll have no problems. That's a lifestyle choice I intend to make.

But these people don't have the option of making a lifestyle choice. I am constantly amazed at the reactions I get to things like my transistor radio. I can't really pick up any station except for the CBC and the local station. They simply won't believe it. There is no abstract thinking in this world, and neither are there any grey areas. What you see is generally what you get.

Charlie is more complex than I ever thought he was. I thought that because he had left to try to make it big but came back because he was homesick, he was a failure. I thought that he was just hiding from life because he had got kicked in the teeth one too many times. But what I understand now is that it takes a bigger man to realize he made the wrong choice—and an even braver man to go back to his home and tell everyone who told him not to go that they were right. I'm not sure I could return home with my tail between my legs and listen to a constant chorus of "I told you so" from those who always knew that I was supposed to be exactly where I started out in the first place.

But Charlie's pretty philosophical about the whole thing. He keeps saying that the teasing doesn't bug him, but I get the feeling he's putting up a brave face.

I sometimes wish my life was that simple.

When the sun finally became too much to ignore, Sandy knew she was going to have to get up and start the day. As much as she would have preferred hiding underneath the covers and pretending the elephant in the room wasn't an issue, she knew she had to make things right with Charlie. She had been angry, and with good reason, but she should never have gone off like she had. Even as she was laying into Charlie, she knew that she was going too far.

Sandy needed to find Charlie, and she needed to do it before she ran out of time.

She came out of her hotel room at the exact moment Mary was walking down the hallway. "Good morning, Sandy. It's good to see you up and about. I hope this mean you're going to go find my brother and talk to him."

"I was never not going to talk to Charlie again. I just needed time. I still think I might need a bit of time, but hiding in my hotel room isn't the answer. I need some air."

"Do you want me to fix you a quick breakfast before you head out?"

"No, thanks. I don't really have too much of an appetite today."

Mary nodded. "I understand that. Stop by the inukshuk if you get a chance on your travels today."

"Why there?"

"It's always been the best place around these parts where you can figure things out."

Sandy chuckled but caught herself almost immediately. She wasn't ready just yet to start feeling better. As she walked out into the sunshine, Sandy let her feet take her wherever it was she was supposed to go. Her mind was flooded with memories of Jack, as per usual. If Sandy was being completely honest with herself, all she could really think about was Tommy, the beautiful little boy with Jack's eyes. The same eyes that had smiled brightly at Sandy on the day they had met. The same eyes that looked stormy whenever Jack was angry at her. The eyes that were usually filled with so much love for Sandy.

The eyes into which Sandy would never look again.

And yet, those eyes were still walking around the planet. But they were supposed to have been on *her* children, not in a boy who had lost both of his parents before he had the chance to know either of them.

Tommy would never get to know Jack. He'd never know the kind of man his father was, how Jack had wanted nothing more than a son to whom he could teach baseball and football and all the things Jack's father had been able to teach him.

But what bothered Sandy even more was that Tommy would never have a half-brother or half-sister to share his secrets with when he needed a friend upon whom he could always rely. He would never be antagonized by a sibling who simply wanted to spend time with him. Tommy would never have the joy of arguing with someone who would always be there for him and love him no matter what.

What a loss for Tommy.

What a loss for Jack.

What a loss for those who loved them both. To not watch Jack's eyes sparkle when his son came into view, or for Tommy to know his father would always love him whether he became rich and powerful or lived a simple life as a handyman.

She'd never get to see it. Sandy knew she shouldn't be taking out her grief on a 4-year-old boy. Tommy could not have controlled his fate any more than Jack could have stopped that driver from running a red light. There were nothing but losers in this situation, and the only option now was to make the best of a terrible situation and find the best way possible to move forward.

Hashing things out with Charlie was only the first step. Although she hadn't been watching exactly where she had been going, Sandy found herself approaching the inukshuk as Mary had suggested. As she got closer, she saw a familiar pickup truck parked beside it. She looked around and finally spotted Charlie sitting on the top of the hill.

Sandy quietly made her way to the hill and walked up to sit beside Charlie. After a few minutes in silence, as Charlie continued to smoke his cigarette, he finally spoke.

"You do realize that it was never about trusting you enough, right?"

Sandy didn't understand what he was trying to tell her.

"Jack not telling you about Tommy. It wasn't because he didn't trust you."

In this moment, Sandy didn't agree. She and Jack had been married, which in her book meant that there was no need to keep anything secret from one another. There should have been no reason to hide anything. But Jack had done just that, and he had kept a secret—a big one. Sandy never thought she had any reason to doubt anything her husband had ever told her. Now she wasn't so sure.

"I suppose I owe you an explanation," Charlie said as he heaved a sigh.

Sandy nodded her head. "I would like to say it's entirely up to you, Charlie, but I do really need an answer. I came here to find out about why Jack loved this place so much, and I find out that the one person who has been helping me is hiding the truth from me."

Charlie nodded. As much as he had been dreading the conversation, he had always known it was a matter of time before it became completely unavoidable. Now that Sandy knew about Tommy, he could avoid it no longer. But finding the words to explain any situation had never been a strength for Charlie, and it was even harder when the conversation involved emotions.

"You already know that I knew Jack. As a matter of fact, he stayed with me."

"Yes. I knew that. It's in his diary. He stayed with you, in your house. You didn't think that was important to me?"

As much as she wanted to know the truth, there was still a small part of her that thought perhaps there was a reason this had remained a secret, and that she didn't really need to know everything. She also feared that her anger would get the best of her, and she would not be able to remain civil while Charlie tried to tell her his side of the story.

Sandy stood up to leave, but Charlie wrapped his hand around her wrist tightly before she could get too far. The anger still coursed through Sandy's eyes as she sat down again.

"I know you're still angry, and you have every right to be, but you are going to have to understand that what I am about to tell you is by no means easy. You'll have to be patient with me."

"Are you going to tell me the whole story?" Sandy asked.

"If you sit there, listen and give me the time I will need to tell the story, then yes."

Slightly embarrassed by her behaviour, Sandy quietly sat back down beside Charlie, folding her hands in her lap. She could see he was having a hard time pulling himself together enough to start talking. As promised, she sat patiently and let Charlie set the pace.

He ran a hand through his hair, heaved a heavy sigh and started to speak. "When I was 19, I felt like my life was going to be about so much more than this town. I told myself that as soon as I had the chance, I would leave for the big city and never come back. As a teenager, I saved every dollar I ever earned doing odd jobs and chores. When I had enough to buy a ticket out of here, I was gone as soon as I could get on that plane."

Before continuing his story, Charlie fumbled around his pockets for his cigarettes and his lighter. Finding both in his left jacket pocket, he pulled out his last cigarette, lit it, and took a few minutes to enjoy it.

"It was the day after my 19th birthday that I left town. For months I had been telling everyone I was leaving and never intended on coming back. They just smiled at me. It was my dad who took me to the airport that day. He had never been much for words, so I wasn't expecting any parting advice from him. All he said was that he completely understood why I had to go. This was important if I was to find my path, and I was always welcome to return when my journey brought me home."

Charlie stood up and began pacing, remembering that was the very last conversation he'd ever had with his father. He still wished he had said so much more that day, but Charlie had always sensed that his father knew what was in his heart. Even though 25 years had passed, Charlie still desperately missed him. His one true regret was that he had been so convinced that leaving everything behind and starting fresh in a big place was where his life was supposed to be, because Charlie was not here at the end.

"Moving to the big city was very difficult in the early stages. I was a kid from a very small, very remote northern community. I had no clue what I was doing, so I will admit having fallen in with the wrong crowd for a bit and getting into a fair bit of trouble in the early going. But I was a pretty big kid and was quick on my feet, so I never really got in over my head. I realized that I was probably headed down the wrong path and straightened myself out. After two months or so, I landed a job at a construction company. I had a tiny bit of experience from working on the odd carpentry and repair job around here, so I had the basic skills I needed to get an entry-level job. I enjoyed the work, enjoyed working with my hands and knew I had found my place."

Sandy quietly pulled out a thermos and two mugs from the satchel she had been carrying. She had asked Mary for some coffee she could take with her, and when Mary had given her more than enough coffee for one person and two mugs, Sandy hadn't questioned it. Now she understood that Mary had hoped this would happen. She poured the coffee and handed the first one to Charlie, who was clearly surprised by the gesture but was thankful nonetheless. He took a long sip and continued his story.

"In those early days in construction, I made friends with a man named Tom. He was a great guy, and we hit it off almost immediately. I thought at first he was just one of the company foremen, because he was pretty laid-back and easy to talk to. After we had gotten to know one another better, I learned that Tom actually owned the company.

"He and I spent a lot of time together, and he took every opportunity to pass along the information and knowledge I needed to know. He helped me slowly move up in the company until I became one of the foremen myself. Things were moving forward, and I was sure that at last I had found my place in the world."

Charlie heaved another sigh.

"Then I got word that my dad was very sick and nearing the end. I knew I would probably never make it back home before he passed, because I was too far away. I was heartbroken, almost sick with grief knowing that I would never see him again. When I told Tom, he said I needed to go back. I reminded him we were in the middle of an important job, but Tom told me that nothing was more important than duty to family in times of need, and I needed to be there. I gathered up all my equipment and headed for the airport. When I arrived and started to explain my situation to the ticket agent, she smiled and handed me a ticket. She then said, 'Tom has taken care of everything, Charlie. You go home and take care of your family.'

"I never did go back to the city after the funeral. I realized all that I needed and all that I loved was here. I managed to get a carpentry job with the town. I met Janet and got married, and we started a family. I soon realized that for as much as I had thought I was supposed to be somewhere else, the life I had always wanted for myself had been right here all along.

"Even though I never returned to work for him, Tom and I stayed in very close communication. We were always exchanging stories about what was happening in our lives, with our children and our hopes for them. Then one day, Tom asked me for a favour. He wanted to send his son to come spend the summer with me up here. Tom said he needed his son to understand about life and could think of no better place, or no better person, to send his son Jack. I told Tom I would be more than happy to have Jack stay in my house for the summer."

And there it was. The one answer Sandy had been wanting the entire time she had been here. She had been looking for that one person who had known Jack, and that person was right under her nose the entire time. She still couldn't fully understand why it was taking Charlie so long to properly explain his relationship with Jack, but Sandy could see the memories were weighing heavy on his heart, and she remained quiet.

"Jack was absolutely miserable his first two weeks here. Apparently he had made some big plans for the summer with his friends, and then his father told him he would be spending the entire summer here with me and my family. His father had not even given him his return plane ticket, so Jack was pretty much stuck here.

"Slowly, Jack began to cheer up. His speech became a little less monosyllabic, and he started to smile. After his first month here, Jack was enjoying himself. One of the main reasons why was that he and my daughter were getting closer."

Charlie reached into the back pocket of his jeans and pulled out his wallet. He opened it up and took out an old photo. He smiled slightly while handing it to Sandy. It was a photograph of a beautiful young woman with long, dark hair and dark eyes almost the colour of dark chocolate. She had a big smile on her face that lit up her features. Even from the old photograph, Sandy could see that this young woman was just as beautiful on the inside.

"She's beautiful, Charlie."

"She sure is. That's Alice, Tommy's mother."

Taking another look, Sandy could definitely see the resemblance between the woman in the photograph and the little boy she had seen run into his grandfather's embrace a few days ago.

"Tell me about her, Charlie. Tell me about Alice and Jack."

"What do you mean? You're the one who has his diary."

Sandy heaved a heavy sigh.

"It's weird, Charlie. He never mentioned her once in his diary. You would think that if she had meant anything to him - and knowing him she did mean something to him - he would have mentioned her at least once.

Charlie was surprised to hear that Alice never came up in any of Jack's entries, but the more he thought about it the more it actually made sense. Jack never spent too much time thinking about or analyzing things while he was here, preferring to spend his time actually enjoying the experience. Thinking back, Charlie never remembered ever seeing Jack actually writing in any kind of notebook while he was here, so he figured that Jack was not documenting his time here, but the thoughts and feeling he needed to think about.

Jack has spent all his time with Alice. There was no need to think about much of anything.

"It was kind of fun watching Alice start liking a boy. I'm not sure she even realized how much her eyes lit up when she was around Jack. When I mentioned it to Janet, she told me to keep it to myself because if Alice knew I was watching she'd get embarrassed and pull back. I kept my mouth shut, and I watched my little girl fall in love with a pretty good kid who seemed to be just as crazy about her. Then near the end of the summer, Jack got word that his father had died, and he needed to get back home immediately. But he didn't want to leave."

Sandy sat up a bit straighter, looking genuinely surprised. "What do you mean, he didn't want to leave? That doesn't sound like Jack at all."

"Not what I meant, Sandy. Jack didn't want to leave because he had a feeling he would never come back here if he did go. Sadly, he was right."

A sad yet comfortable silence fell over both Sandy and Charlie. Each had fallen back into their own memories of Jack, feeling the depth of his loss all over again. For Charlie, it was the first time in a very long time he had talked to anyone about Alice. Here, everyone knew what was happening in a little less than two hours, so nothing was really a secret. After something happened, no one ever needed to talk about it again.

"And as to the reason why you never heard about Alice until now, think about it - you know Jack was the kind of guy who never wanted to over-think anything if he could avoid it. He never spent all that much time looking back, and analysis wasn't the thing that kept him going. He wouldn't have wanted to pull apart everything about what happened with Alice while he was here, because that would have taken away so much from the experience."

"But he loved analyzing things, Charlie. He never stopped rehashing experiences. So why not this one?"

"Come on, Sandy. You knew him better than anyone. You know the answer. He knew he could never come back. Why would he want to spend his time thinking about something he couldn't have?"

Finally, Sandy, understood why Jack found this place so special and important. In a way, Sandy knew she had been lucky. If there had been no reason for him to have left so suddenly, Jack may have never left Alice, and then Sandy would have never met him. Thoughts of Alice being left behind soon followed with thoughts about Tommy, and Sandy realized Jack and Alice's story hadn't been completely told.

"Charlie, did Alice know she was pregnant before Jack left?"

Charlie had been dreading the telling of the next part of the story, and he sighed yet again before he continued. "Alice had absolutely no idea she was pregnant when Jack left. It wasn't until three months after he was gone that she began having symptoms. Alice told Janet first, and they told me together. She kept apologizing to me, telling me she was sorry for what she had done. I told her she had done nothing wrong, and we would deal with whatever happened together.

"She must have been so relieved when you said that to her, Charlie. That is what makes you a great man and no doubt a great grandfather to Tommy," Sandy said. "How did Jack react when he found out?"

Charlie shook his head and smiled. "He started apologizing almost immediately. He swore up and down that he'd never meant for anything like this to happen, that they had only been together a few times and had been careful, and that he had never taken advantage of my daughter. None of what he said surprised me, not even when he told me he didn't think there was any way he could come back to take care of Alice and his unborn child."

"Why did he think he couldn't come back?"

Charlie hesitated a bit, and Sandy knew she probably needed to brace herself for another shock. She wasn't all that certain she could deal with yet another bombshell from her dead husband's past. Charlie pulled a crumpled envelope from his pocket and held it out to Sandy. Almost immediately she recognized the handwriting on the front of the envelope. It was a letter from Jack.

"Another letter, Charlie? I'm not sure I really want to read anything more from Jack right now."

"You need to read this one, Sandy. Trust me."

Sandy hesitantly took the envelope and pulled out the letter inside.

Chapter 20

I always told Charlie he would know what to do with this letter and when he needed to give it to someone. I'm not even sure what to say here. I just know I need to say something.

We've never met—and we may never meet, if I'm being completely honest—but you hold a piece of my heart in yours.

You have to understand that we all have choices to make in our lives, and we also must live with them. In some cases, the choices are very east; in other cases, the choices are heart-wrenching. The choice I made when it came to you was the hardest decision I have ever had to make, or ever will.

My life was largely out of my control when I heard of your birth. Even before your creation, I had few choices I could make on my own. A great deal of what was to be my life was already predestined even before I was born.

Not that I'm making excuses for never trying to meet you. I always figured it would be better if we never met. I knew that if I ever saw you, I would have given up everything in my life, destroying your life and mine in one fell swoop. That wouldn't be fair to you, because I know your life with Charlie and Janet was a good one.

If Charlie has not told you, your mother was his daughter. She was too good for me, and I'll never know what it was she saw in me, but she probably saved my life. She helped me see that in every situation there is good and there is bad, so we should accept it for what it is. She showed me that we are our choices, and we must hold our heads high.

I had a life to return to, and I could not disappoint those I had left behind who were counting on my return. I knew I had to go, and your mother fully understood and supported me.

I hope you have a good life. I hope you have a happy life. I hope you know how you are loved. And I hope you can forgive me for staying away, because in the end, I did it for you.

Be true to yourself and you'll never be sorry. I know I'm not.

Jack

Sandy said, "Oh, god. He never came back because of me. This is my fault."

"Stop it. You know Jack well enough to know he was his own man. He made his own choices, and he stuck by them." Sandy shook her head, but Charlie knew she wasn't convinced just yet. "His mother still needed him to help with his father's affairs. Jack was so deeply entangled in things almost immediately upon his return home, and there were no other options. Alice and Jack talked about everything for a very long time. By the end of the conversation, they had both decided that although he couldn't come back, Jack would do everything in his power to make sure Alice and his child never wanted for anything, and he more than kept his word."

It was in that statement that Sandy understood how this place had helped to shaped the man that Jack would become—the man that she had fallen in love with, the man she knew she would spend the rest of her life mourning.

"How did Alice deal with being a single mother?" she asked.

"She was fantastic. I should say that although Jack wasn't here to help her out, Alice was never on her own. She had more support than she ever thought possible from Mary and Janet, and I gave her all the love and support I could. When Tommy was born, I could not have been more proud of my little girl. She had a peaceful, gentle delivery, and the love she had for her son was clear from the first moment she held him.

"That's when things started to go wrong. Alice's blood pressure dropped dangerously low, but the nurses were able to stabilize her. A few hours later, the decision was made to send Alice to Inuvik. Janet and I took Tommy with us, and we accompanied Alice on the flight out. While we were waiting on Alice, Tommy got his first check-up by a doctor and passed with flying colours. But Alice fell into a coma and slipped away. She never held Tommy a second time."

Sandy quickly brushed the tears from her cheeks. She now felt even worse for the anger she had directed at Charlie for not having been completely honest with her about knowing Jack.

Charlie cleared his throat and continued the story. "Janet and I immediately realized we had to take Tommy. There was no question that we were going to raise our grandson. I knew I was going to have to tell Jack about Alice. When I called to tell him, he was heartbroken. He said that Alice had stayed in close contact throughout the entire pregnancy, and they had chosen the name Tommy together, after his father. As much as he knew he should step up and take responsibility for his son, Jack realized that Tommy would be so much better off here with his grandparents, who already adored him and would give him a fantastic life. Besides, he mentioned that he had just met a fantastic girl at school, and although it was still early, he thought that she could be the one to spend his life with."

Sandy's heart shattered into a million pieces yet again. She also felt more than a little guilty, as if she had been the reason Jack had never met his son.

"Don't blame yourself for any choices that Jack made, Sandy. You and I both know he made the choices he thought were right, and he never blamed anyone else for how things went in his life. Besides, I know for a fact he was going to tell you the truth pretty soon."

"What do you mean, Charlie?"

He heaved a heavy sigh. "I'm not even sure if I should tell you this, because I think it's only going to hurt you, but I don't think keeping it to myself is a good idea either."

"I hope you know you can tell me anything, and whatever it is, I'll keep it between us if that's what you want."

Charlie still remained quiet. The longer he didn't say anything, the more anxious Sandy became. Whatever this big secret was, the conflict Charlie was having with his conscience was intense.

Finally, Charlie said, "I did hear from Jack. He called me about six months ago."

"You're kidding! Jack called you out of the blue after years of silence? What did he say? How did he explain why it had taken him this long to contact you?"

"He told me he was planning a surprise for someone close to him."

"Who?"

Charlie heaved another sigh. "He wanted to arrange an anniversary gift for you."

"Me? What was he planning? Why would he call you to ..." Sandy stopped mid-sentence. She knew exactly why Jack had called someone he hadn't spoken to since the day he'd left Holman.

He'd written in his letter with the journal that he had always wanted to take her to Holman to visit the one place that had changed his life, that had made him into the man who had stopped to help her change a flat tire and tried to keep her mind off the fact she was stuck at school on Christmas Eve.

Jack had written that he wanted to show her one day.

"He was going to bring me here, wasn't he?" Sandy whispered, the pain in her voice almost palpable.

Charlie nodded. "It was supposed to be a surprise. He told me that it was time to bring the most important person in his life to the most important place in his life."

Sandy couldn't stay strong any longer. She had been fighting to keep her wits about her all day, and when she finally realized Jack had been ready to share this part of his life with her, there was nothing in the world that could keep her walls from crumbling She broke down, weeping once again for the loss of the one true love in her life.

Unbuttoning his left front shirt pocket, Charlie pulled out a second folded envelope and handed it to Sandy. When she took a closer look, Sandy recognized Jack's handwriting.

Chapter 21

Charlie,

I am sure you never expected in a million years to hear from me again. Not that I never wanted to stay in touch, but in some ways I always thought it would be easier for both of us if I remained nothing more than a memory, for so many reasons.

You know how important my time in Holman was, and how much it changed me for the better. You also know there were things that happened that summer that changed the course of many lives—and I'm not sure if it was for the good of everyone. But choices were made, and everyone had to live with the consequences.

Charlie, I never meant to stay away so long. I had always intended to come back for a visit, but I always thought there would be a "perfect time."

I've realized now there is never a perfect time. You have to make the time for the things you feel are important. You are the only person who can determine exactly when is the right time.

So, now is the time.

It's time to tell Sandy the one secret I have left to share, and I can't think of a better way than to show her. I am working a planning a trip to Holman. I want her to see the place for herself. I want her to understand the deepest part of me. Not that she doesn't already know me, but I feel as if it's time to lay myself completely bare.

I want her to experience what I did, see the places I saw, meet the people who changed my life for the better. The people and places that helped *me become the man that was worthy enough for someone like her (although I don't think that's at all possible).*

She's spectacular, Charlie. Wondrous. Amazing. More than I could have ever hopes for in my life. In sharing Holman with her, there will be no part of me she will not know about me—and that thought is so freeing.

To say that I love her isn't giving enough power or emotion to the feeling I have for her, Charlie. Just wait until you meet her, and you will understand completely.

I'll be in touch soon to work out the final details. Until then, start thinking about how I can give my wife the experience of a lifetime.

Your friend always,
Jack

Sandy quietly refolded the letter and put it back in the envelope. Sitting in complete silence, she could almost hear the pieces of her broken heart snapping back into place in her chest.

Charlie gave Sandy a few minutes. He had a feeling Jack's words could not have come at a better time. All Charlie could do was wrap his arms around her and wait until the tears ended

"I wanted you to never forget how much Jack really loved you, Sandy. I hoped to show you all the things that he wanted to show you himself while the two of you were here."

Sandy could only nod. Jack never failed to surprise her—and probably never would. Charlie had once again brought them a little bit closer.

"You have no idea how much you have done for me, Charlie. I could never explain it, but you have helped me heal the massive hole in my heart. I know Jack would thank you for taking such good care of his wife, even after he's gone."

Chapter 22

After spending six weeks in Holman, Sandy knew that she was ready to go back and take the next step in starting a life without Jack.

She'd had the time to properly mourn her husband. She'd found some inner peace and the strength to go on without him. Moving on would never be easy, and she knew there would be a hole in her heart that could never be repaired, but she also knew there was no choice. As much as she wanted to curl up into a ball and have herself buried in the cold, hard ground next to Jack, Sandy realized that she had to live for Jack.

She knew she couldn't keep hiding from what her life was now, yet she hesitated about having to return to an empty house and a lonely bed. Without Jack, Sandy could see no good reason why she had to go back.

But she wasn't ready to leave everything behind just yet. There were things Sandy would need to do, and people she knew she would have to talk to before she could make any sort of changes. If she was going to be completely honest with herself and everyone in her life, she owed them an explanation. What she was going to say was still a mystery, but she had a three-day trip in front of her to decide.

The drive to the airport was a quiet one, with Charlie and Janet escorting Sandy on her way home. Sandy didn't expect such a send-off from her new friends, yet she wasn't surprised either. There was a bond created during her time here that had in fact been forged one summer when a young man was forced to spend an entire summer in a corner of the country he never expected to see in his lifetime. Jack had been the foundation for the friendship, but her own experience would keep Sandy from forgetting about her Northern friends.

No one had yet to say a word, and Sandy knew that someone was going to have to speak. "Looks like the rest of week is going to be pretty nice."

Charlie stifled a chuckle because he knew exactly what Sandy was trying to do. "Yeah," he said. "But that doesn't mean it's not time to get ready for snow. I've got a feeling it will be here before we know it."

"You think so?"

Janet nodded her agreement. "He's usually not wrong about these things, Sandy. As long as I've known Charlie, his predictions about the weather have been spot-on."

"You're kidding, right?"

Janet chuckled. "I wish I were, Sandy. He's got some sort of sixth sense when it comes to the weather. His father was cursed with the same thing."

Silence reigned over the trio once again. Sandy had hoped there would be more conversation once the weather had been fully discussed, but it did not seem to flow freely. She knew she was holding back, but she also knew that if she were to start, there would be no way to keep her emotions in check, and getting on the plane with puffy eyes wasn't an attractive option right now.

She turned to look at Charlie. "You know, I'll never be able to thank you enough for the gift you've given me."

"That goes both ways. I had always wondered what had become of Jack after he left Holman, and thanks to you, I know he had a good life."

Sandy quickly brushed a tear from her cheek. "And thanks to you, I spent my life with a great man. I only hope he was as happy as I was."

"If the time I've spent with you was any indication of the person you have been since the day he met you, I'll bet he was one of the happiest men on this planet."

Sandy smiled through the tears. Janet, who up until this point had kept quiet, wrapped an arm around Sandy's shoulders. She had found a new friend in Sandy—one Janet feared she might never see again. The memories would remain and the remembered stories would become a part of their histories, but Sandy had a sinking feeling that if she did actually leave she would never return.

"This place will never be the same without you around, Sandy," Janet said.

"You've lived this long without me, Janet," Sandy said. "I think you'll be able to keep on going when I'm gone."

"Don't sell yourself short. You've resolved an important part of the past for both of us. Wondering what Jack had become was one of those questions that gnawed away at the back of our minds since the day we took him to the airport. Now that we've had some sort of closure, we can remember the good memories of that time and know that he lived a good life."

Sandy began to weep openly. She had known that this path would lead to a scene, but she had hoped to have some control over the waterworks. Obviously, she had no control whatsoever. She was weeping like a baby. The reality of the situation was too much to bear. Jack had never returned to visit his friends; Sandy wondered whether this was to be her future as well.

All Charlie could do was wrap his arms around his new friend. He was trying hard to keep the tears from his eyes, but after fighting a losing battle, Charlie began to weep too. He wept for the old friend he would never see again, and for the new one he was watching leave him behind to go back to her own life.

Janet was crying just as hard as Sandy, if not harder. She had few female friends in Holman, and having Sandy around for the past month and a half had been wonderful. Now that Sandy was going back to resume her own life, Janet was already feeling the void.

"You know you can't stay away for years like Jack did, don't you?" Janet said.

Sandy smiled weakly. "Somehow I had a feeling one of you would say that."

"She's right, Sandy. I lost touch with Jack, and now it's too late to catch up with him. I'm not about to find out from someone else that you died with us ever seeing you again."

"I guess we've both learned that waiting for the perfect time doesn't happen in real life, so you've got to take your chances when they come up. I promise you both that the first chance I get to come back here, I'll take it without hesitation."

"You've got our phone number," Janet said. "You call us the minute you want to come back. That bedroom will be waiting for you. I might have even finished the repairs on my parents' house by the time you come back."

"Maybe next time I come back, we might actually catch something when we go out fishing, eh, Charlie?"

Charlie chuckled and then pulled Sandy tighter into his embrace. Just then, the pre-boarding announcement boomed over the public address system. Sandy slowly pulled away from Charlie and made her way to the gate, not daring to look back. Once the general boarding announcement came, Sandy stopped as she heard a surprising voice coming from behind her.

"I hope you have a good trip back home," Peter said.

Sandy turned around and faced Peter. Of all the people she had thought she might see on the day she left Holman, Peter was the last one on the list. "What brings you by? Did you come to make sure I was really leaving town?"

"I guess I deserved that one," Peter said, chuckling. "I just wanted to come see you off—and to tell you I'm sorry I was so nasty to you when we first met at the co-op. I'm sure Charlie has told you that we've seen more than our fair share of people come and go in this town, and I put you in the category of people looking for nothing more than to be able to say they came to Holman and were here a few days."

Sandy heard Peter's words, but she wasn't sure whether he was being sincere or playing another awful joke on her. They had not spent much time together during her stay in Holman, but other people had told her that Peter had been her harshest critic, and he never missed an opportunity to badmouth her and tell people he didn't think she had any reason to be here in Holman, so she should just go back to when she came from.

"You really haven't had much that was good to say about me, Peter. In fact, I'm trying to figure out if you're being sincere right now, or if you're just setting me up for some kind of cruel trick. Because if you're setting me up, I'm going to be pretty mad at you."

"I'm not setting you up, Sandy. I mean it. I was wrong about you."

"What made you change your mind?"

Peter nodded toward Janet. "Janet's my niece. I'm a pretty stubborn son of a gun—everyone around here knows it. I usually make a decision about a first impression pretty quickly, and usually that don't change. I'm somewhat of a legend for that way of living, but it's gotten me this far without steering me wrong. But in your case, I'm about to make a big change. I was wrong about you, and for that I apologize."

Sandy was stunned. Of all the things she expected to get out of this last day in Holman, an apology from Peter was nowhere close to being on the list. She knew she could play around with him and drag this out longer than necessary, but Sandy realized she didn't want things to end on a bad note.

"I'll tell you what, Peter. I wasn't expecting an apology from you, because I thought you didn't have much to say about me and there would never be anything to change your mind. It hurt at first, but then I realized that I can't expect everyone to like me, and that you probably had your own reasons for not liking me. But I'm glad you came around. I wanted every memory of my time in Holman to be a good one, and now I know that will be possible, because I know you do like me and understand my reasons for coming here and finding the answers I was looking for."

"Janet told me everything. She explained why you were here and what you were hoping to find. I only hope you did find the answers."

Sandy nodded, not trusting the strength of her voice. She had overcome the last obstacle in her way. She had found the answers she needed to find the strength to move forward, and she had made one more new friend.

"I'm glad you found the resolution you were looking for, Sandy. Everyone deserves that much in her life."

Her journey here was now complete.

Then came the final boarding announcement for the plane back to Sandy's old life—the one she would now have to face with the knowledge that she would never be able to live it again.

She turned around and ran straight back into Charlie's embrace. "I'm coming back, Charlie. I swear I'm coming back." She brushed a tear from her cheek, leaned over and kissed Charlie. Without another word, Sandy hugged Janet quickly and then ran for her waiting plane.

She never looked back and spent her entire trip to Inuvik weeping silently.

Chapter 23

For the first few days, adjusting to the pace of her old life in the city was difficult for Sandy. After having spent six weeks in a town that didn't worry about being on time, many people couldn't reconcile some of Sandy's newly acquired habits. Some people had thought she was crazy for dropping everything and running off to the Arctic for six weeks, and her behaviour since she had returned was proof that something was wrong with her. For Sandy, she knew she had never felt more right.

Regardless of what people were saying to her face or behind her back, Sandy wasn't the same person who had run off. Back then, she was an emotional and physical mess. Even thought she had been gone for a short time, that time away from her everyday schedule had been a godsend. By having the chance to get another perspective on things, Sandy was able to find the time to heal properly and find the strength to live again.

Being back in a big city was more difficult than Sandy had expected. Sandy had discovered a new way of living, a way that didn't rely on who was making the most money or having everything happen instantaneously, but on how to live one's life as honestly as possible. Until her visit to Holman, Sandy had thought that reality only existed in the movies or in her fantasy world.

None of her friends understood her fixation on Holman; they had expected her to come back and pick up where she had left things. Not that they expected her to be the person she was, but they at least hoped she would have found a way to move forward with her life.

Sandy had also been dreading the day when Jack's diary would be finished. She'd read the rest of it, but when it came time to read the very last entry, there was something that kept Sandy from going any further. Jack's story was all she had left.

And Sandy knew that is exactly why she couldn't finish it. Once she reached the very last line on the very last page, there would be nothing left of her life with Jack but her memories. When there were no more entries to read, she would have to move forward—alone.

She'd actually hesitated about reading the final entry in Jack's diary for three weeks. Although the diary never left her sight since the first day she'd found it, reading the final entry was a step she wasn't prepared to take.

She wasn't ready to live a life without her husband.

Everyone knew she was prolonging the inevitable. Her friends knew she never went anywhere without the diary, and when they asked her if she was finished reading it, Sandy's weak excuses told everyone what they already knew.

Sandy couldn't let Jack go.

It was Alison who finally pushed her to finish reading. As much as she knew Sandy would be heartbroken when there were no more words from Jack, Alison knew her best friend had to find the strength to move on and let go of him. There would be no ideal time for this conversation, so Alison decided she would have to be the one to bring up the subject. One afternoon when Sandy had invited her over for coffee, Alison knew she had to take the chance and risk breaking her best friend's heart one more time.

"So," Alison said. "Have you finished it yet?"

"Finished what, Allie?"

"You know exactly what I'm talking about, Sandy. Have you finished reading it yet?"

No," Sandy said curtly. "And you know damn well why."

"I have a pretty good idea, but why don't you tell me, and I can see if I'm right."

"I can't finish it," Sandy whispered.

"What?"

Sandy stood up and took her cup to the sink. "You know damn well what I said! I can't finish it! If I read that last entry ..."

She couldn't finish the sentence. Fighting hard to maintain her composure, Sandy knew it was a fight she would ultimately lose.

Alison knew exactly what was going on, and moved towards Sandy. "You can't finish reading it, because you know the minute you finish reading, your life with him can't continue. The minute there are no more entries to read, he'll be gone forever, and there's no way you will get him back."

When she heard the words, Sandy couldn't hold her emotions in check any longer. Breaking into tears, she grabbed blindly for something to hold on to and found comfort in her best friend's arms. A few minutes after completely breaking down, Sandy found her voice was once again working.

"What am I going to do, Allie? I know I have to move on with my life, but I don't know if I'm strong enough to go on without Jack. And I can't begin to move forward until I settle everything, which means I have to read the last entry. But I'm afraid, and I've been reading the same entry over and over. I can't even turn the page to look at the last entry."

Alison moved her hand to Sandy's face to brush an errant strand of hair from her forehead. "Listen to me. You are the strongest woman I know. I know you're terrified to try and live a life without Jack, but your inability to move forward is killing you. You can't stay like this. I know you don't want to live like this, and I know for damn sure Jack would not want you to live like this."

Sandy brushed away the few last remaining tears from her face. She knew Alison was right: in order to move on with her life, she was going to have to say goodbye to the man who had been her life up until this point.

"I can't do this alone," Sandy said.

Alison reached out for Sandy's hand. "I'm not about to let my best friend do this alone either. You and I are going to sit here and read the final entry together. Then you are going to cry for your husband, and I am going to sit here and hold you until the tears stop. Then you and I are going to find a way to get you to move on without him."

Sandy heaved a sigh of relief, even though her tears had already begun to fall. She squeezed Alison's hand and then sat at the kitchen table. This was going to be the hardest thing she had ever done, but she could not keep from taking the next step, because Jack would never forgive her for not being able to move forward.

Heaving another sigh, Sandy opened her husband's diary for what she knew would be the last time.

So here it is. My last day in Holman.

Three months ago, this day couldn't get here quick enough.

Now that this day has finally arrived, I almost wish I could go back and do it all over again. I want to relive every minute and find a reason to enjoy the times I didn't enjoy because I was too busy trying to find reasons to hate this place.

I know if I had a second chance, I'd love every minute I spent in Holman. I'd relive the long days spent out on the land. I'd relive the brisk wind that blew even in the middle of July. I'd relive the enormous bugs. I'd even relive the loneliness and silence I suffered through when I first got here.

Because even as I suffered through my most profound loneliness, I learned something very important. I learned that although I am very happy spending time on my own, it is still important to connect with other people from time to time. I learned that I know more about life and what I want from it that I ever realized. I learned that I'm not a bad person.

And I learned that there is much more to life and what one should want from it than I have ever understood sitting in my parents' house or in my classes. I've learned that there are people who might not be as well-educated as I will some but who are infinitely smarter than I will ever be.

My father was right to send me here. He knew that I needed to see a new part of the world and experience a different life from the privilege I have always been fortunate enough to enjoy thanks to both my parents. I have realized that regardless of how unfair things seem at the time, I have been given so much more than I actually deserve.

And that is probably the most important lesson I leave here with: Whatever I receive in my life is a gift, and I should be thankful for the things I do have, and not envy people for the things I want.

As I leave this place that I have been lucky enough to call home (even if only for a short while), I know that I will be forever tied to this place. Even if I never step foot in Holman or anywhere north of Thunder Bay, a piece of my soul will always be here, awaiting my return. Charlie says that there are two kinds of people in the world: those who love the North, and those who hate it. He says that people generally give themselves away pretty quickly, and he was sure I was going to be a hater of the North. He was genuinely surprised to discover that I actually held a deep affection and respect for it. He even went as far as to insinuate that he wouldn't be surprised to see me back in two years.

That isn't to say I won't ever come back. Perhaps in a few years, once I have finished my degree and have found the person I will spend the rest of my life with. Maybe then I will find a reason to come back. I would want that person to know everything there is to know about me, and that will be an experience of a lifetime.

Maybe I'll even send my son up here for the summer.

They had been sitting in silence for nearly 10 minutes. Jack's diary was now finished. From what Alison could tell, the reality of the situation had not yet sunk in for Sandy. In fact, there was no reaction whatsoever from Sandy, which worried Alison even more.

There was no doubt that Sandy would never be without Jack; Alison knew that much. The best friend she had ever known, who had laughed with her in the good times and cried with her in the bad times, was gone forever. In many ways, Alison was mourning a huge loss in her own life. Although Alison may have lost a friend as she once was, not a soul mate, the pain was just as real. Alison wanted Sandy to react, but she was too frightened to move a muscle. She wasn't sure she would know what to do if Sandy went to pieces, and she doubted her ability to put her friend's heart back together.

Suddenly, Sandy began to laugh. Alison knew this was the beginning of the fallout, but she didn't know how long it would go on.

"I'm still here," Sandy whispered.

Alison was taken aback. Was she supposed to say something? Should she just wait for Sandy to continue? Before she could make a decision, Sandy continued talking.

"I'll bet you're thinking I've lost my mind, breaking into laughter like that. I think I probably have, but for some strange reason I've never been more sane."

"Are you sure? I wasn't expecting this from you. An emotional breakdown, sure—but not joyous laughter."

"Let's see if I can explain this," Sandy said. "I was sure I wasn't strong enough to go on without Jack. I wasn't even sure I *wanted* to go on without him."

"You can't give up, Sandy. You know that is not what Jack would have wanted."

"I know. And that's why I started laughing. I suddenly realized that Jack had helped me find the strength to go on without him, even if he wasn't really here."

"Okay, you've lost me."

"Jack's diary helped me through. I've been carrying it with me and reading it since the day I found it. Jack's been gone for more than six months, but it's taken me this long to be ready to move forward. Don't you think it's a pretty wild coincidence that I'm ready to move on just as I reach the last page?"

"You're saying Jack is guiding you through your grieving process."

Sandy smiled. "In his own way. He gave me something to hold on to when I had nothing else. Think about it: what have I been doing since Jack died?"

"Reading his diary," Alison said, finally beginning to understand her friend's logic.

"Exactly. Almost every single day since he's been gone, I've been spending time with Jack—his thoughts, his passages, his experiences, who he was before I ever met him."

Alison understood that Sandy was right. The only way that she could have survived was with Jack's help. Yet again, Alison found herself envying Sandy and her relationship with her husband, because their connection had survived even through death.

"So what now? Are you ready to go on without him?"

Sandy shrugged. "To be honest, I'm not really sure. I know that whatever happens, Jack will always be an enormous part of my life. But I know that I can go on without him and be okay. He may be dead, but this proves he's not gone. He's given me the best gift he could have given me: time to heal."

That was the moment Alison knew the Sandy who had been married to Jack was gone forever. The new Sandy was strong enough to move forward with her life, but she would always have a hole in her soul no one would ever fill. Sandy wouldn't grow old with her soul mate, but she had been given enough time to find the courage to survive.

And she'd be okay.

"So, what are you going to do with Jack's diary now?"

Sandy took a deep breath. "I'm going to burn it."

If Alison had been confused earlier by Sandy's laughter, she was now completely lost. The diary had meant so much to Sandy since the day she had found it, and Alison couldn't believe that she now wanted to let the diary go. "I don't understand."

"I don't need to hold on to the diary to be able to hold on to my memories," Sandy explained. "I'll always carry Jack's memories with me."

"But don't you think burning your last link to Jack is a little extreme?"

"Not really. He's always going to be with me, Allie. It doesn't matter where I am; Jack is always nearby."

Alison smiled. "Are you trying to tell you're being haunted by your dead husband?"

"Not quite," Sandy said, chuckling. "But his spirit is always around. And whatever happens, I think Jack will always be around, watching out for me. I don't want to hold on to the past with physical things. I want to celebrate it through my memories."

Alison got out of her chair and walked over to the cupboards. She opened one over the stove and pulled out an old aluminum mixing bowl and a box of wooden matches. Returning to the kitchen table, she placed the bowl in front of Sandy and handed her the box of matches.

Sandy hesitated. She was ready to talk about moving forward, but actually moving forward was an entirely different matter. Would she be able to follow through with this ceremony, or would she find out she wasn't as strong as everyone seemed to think she was? But she knew in her heart that this was the right thing to do, and she could almost feel Jack looking down on her, giving her the support she needed.

Finally, she took a deep breath, closed her eyes and took the matches. Sandy opened the box and pulled out a match. By this point, she was fighting the tears welling up her eyes, and she silently prayed her vision would stay clear enough for her to light the match without setting Alison's kitchen on fire.

"You can do this, Sandy," Alison said gently, sensing her friend needed to hear the words now. "If you can't do it for your own reasons, just remember that Jack doesn't want you living in the past. You've got to move on because that's what he would want you to do."

The sound of the match striking the box was the only sound in the room. As she picked up Jack's diary, Sandy whispered a prayer. She lit the corners of the diary, watching the flame spread across its leather cover and through the pages inside. Once she could no longer hold on to the diary, Sandy dropped it into the bowl and watched flames ultimately consume her last tangible connection to Jack.

The tears now ran freely down her cheeks as well as Alison's. Neither one dared to speak a word as they watched the diary burn, but Sandy was the one who found her voice first.

"I'm going back, Allie."

"Back? Back where?"

"Holman. I need to be there. I've already organized everything at work. They've given me a leave of absence and told me there will always be a job for me when I come back here. But to be quite honest, I don't think I'll ever go back to work there again. Right now, I'm just prolonging the inevitable."

"What about your house? You haven't sold it, have you?"

"My nephew Josh is going to live in it," Sandy said. "He's going to university in the fall, and since he needs a place to stay, I told him he was more than welcome to stay as long as he wants. But you have probably already figured out that I can't live in the house anymore either. There are far too many ghosts, and everywhere I turn, I see Jack. I can't live like that. But I'm also not ready to let someone else live in our house other than Josh. I know he will take the best care possible of my house, because he knew how much I loved Jack, and I trust Josh to honour his uncle's memory. Besides, every young university student should have a great place to live while he's going to school," Sandy said with a slight smile on her face.

Alison began to panic. Every base had been covered, and there was a plan for every contingency. From the way Sandy was talking, her friend wasn't going to be back anytime soon. "You're not coming back, are you?" Alison said quietly. Her heart was beginning to break.

"I didn't hear you," Sandy said.

Alison heaved a sigh. "I said, you're not coming back, are you?"

Sandy put her coffee cup down. As she looked into Alison's eyes, she realized she wasn't being fair. Although she was ready to leave her life with Jack behind without a great deal of hesitation, Sandy had to make room for those who had been part of her former life in her new life without her husband. "Alison, you will always be a huge part of my life. No matter where I go or how long we are apart, you will always be my closest friend. There is no way I could have made it through these past few months without your support, and I know I relied on you more often than I should have. But I have to go. This is the right thing for me to do. I am starting a new phase of my life, and I can't start it here in a house filled with memories of Jack. In time, I'll be able to come back and live in this world again, but right now I have to go as far away as possible to heal my heart, my soul and my spirit. But I promise you: I'll come back to you, Allie. I swear to God I will."

Alison put down her cup of coffee to take a long, hard look at her best friend. If there had been some way to convince Sandy not to go and leave everything behind, she would have laid it out for Sandy to think about. Judging by the look on Sandy's face, there was no room for argument.

Any attempt to get Sandy to stay would have been selfish. In watching her friend work through her grief and her pain, Alison had grown to admire her even more. Now with Jack's diary completed, Alison knew Sandy had to leave everything and go back, because that was where she needed to be. Whatever else she knew, Alison knew her friend had to leave, and she wasn't about to stop her.

"So," Alison said, hoping she seemed nonchalant, "when does your flight leave?"

Getting off the plane in Holman this time, Sandy felt more at home than lost. She immediately began to relax as she caught sight of the Arctic Ocean, and she took a deep breath of fresh air. She could feel Jack's presence stronger than it had been in weeks.

Once she had collected her luggage, Sandy took a seat in the terminal to wait for her ride. She had told Charlie what time her flight was coming in, but because he was back doing work for the housing corporation, he wasn't too sure if he'd be able to pick her up. He promised he'd find someone to come get her if he could not.

Her trip had been long and exhausting. Flying wasn't something she particularly enjoyed under the best of conditions, and flying to the Arctic was certainly not the best of conditions. She closed her eyes and enjoyed the silence.

Suddenly she heard a familiar voice call out.

"You're new to the North, aren't you?"

Although she didn't open her eyes, a smile crossed Sandy's face.

"Are you talking to me?"

"Well, you're the only person who didn't have someone waiting for them when the plane landed," Charlie said. "I would have been here sooner, but I had to finish repairing a roof before it started to rain."

Sandy chuckled and then opened her eyes to find her friend standing before her. "Hey, Charlie. I missed you."

"This place hasn't been the same without you," he said. "Janet has been making all sorts of preparations to the house for you."

"Are you sure you want me to move into your house again?"

"Janet and I have moved into my parents' house now. You'll have the whole house to yourself. Besides, we'll feel better knowing someone is living in the place."

Sandy smiled. She knew her time here would be a good one, no matter how long she stayed.

It was then that Sandy noticed Charlie had brought along another person as part of the welcoming committee. Tommy had been standing off to the side watching his grandfather interact with this new person.

"Tommy, come over here and meet my friend Sandy." Cautiously, the little boy came closer.

Sandy smiled and stretched out her hand. "Hi Tommy. My name's Sandy. Your grandfather here has told me a lot about you."

Tommy remained quiet until Charlie pushed him to say something. "My grandpa says you knew my dad."

Tears immediately sprang to Sandy's eyes, and she nodded. "Yes. I knew your dad really well, Tommy. You look a lot like him."

"Really? Did he like baseball too?"

"He sure did. But he liked football even more. I would love to tell you more stories about your dad, if you'll let me."

"My grandpa says you're going to be staying in our old house. Can I come over and visit my old bedroom?"

Sandy smiled brightly. "You can come visit me whenever you want, Tommy."

Charlie cleared his throat, the emotion quite evident. "Come on, kiddo. Let's bring Sandy back to the house. Your grandma's been cooking all day for her arrival."

Tommy nodded excitedly and ran out towards the pickup. Finally, Sandy turned and wrapped her arms around Charlie. "It's good to be back here, Charlie."

Charlie pulled back to look into Sandy's eyes and smiled. "Welcome home, Sandy. Welcome home."

Printed in the United States
By Bookmasters